THE

NORTON SCORES

An Anthology for Listening

Fourth Edition • Expanded

Volume 1

THE

NORTON SCORES

An Anthology for Listening

FOURTH EDITION • EXPANDED
IN TWO VOLUMES

VOLUME I:
GREGORIAN CHANT TO BEETHOVEN

EDITED BY

ROGER KAMIEN

W · W · NORTON & COMPANY
New York · London

Acknowledgments

The text translations for items 2, 5, 6, and 12 are by Dr. Yvette Louria.
The text translation for item 13 is by Albert Seay.

ISBN 0-393-95304-1

Page makeup and highlighting by Roberta Flechner.
PRINTED IN THE UNITED STATES OF AMERICA.
Library of Congress Cataloging in Publication Data
Main entry under title:
The Norton scores.
    Includes index.
    Contents: v. 1. Gregorian chant to Beethoven—v. 2. Schubert to Glass.
    1. Music appreciation—Music collections.   I. Kamien, Roger.
MT6.5.N7   1984b   83-19428

W. W. Norton & Company, Inc., 500 Fifth Avenue, New York, N. Y. 10110
W. W. Norton & Company Ltd., 37 Great Russell Street, London WC1B 3NU
    6 7 8 9 0

Contents

Preface

This anthology is designed for use in introductory music courses, where the ability to read music is not a prerequisite. The unique system of highlighting employed in this book enables students to follow full orchestral scores after about one hour of instruction. This system also has the advantage of permitting students who *can* read music to perceive every aspect of the score. It is felt that our system of highlighting will be of greater pedagogical value than artificially condensed scores, which restrict the student's vision to pre-selected elements of the music. The use of scores in introductory courses makes the student's listening experience more intense and meaningful, and permits the instructor to discuss music in greater depth.

The works included in this Fourth Edition have been chosen from among those most frequently studied in introductory courses. The selections range from Gregorian chant to the present day, and represent a wide variety of forms, genres, and performing media. To make this Fourth Edition reflect today's concert repertory more closely, increased emphasis has been placed on instrumental and secular music of earlier periods and on music of the present century. A majority of the pieces are given in their entirety, while the others are represented by complete movements or sections particularly suitable for classroom study. Scenes from operas and some choral works are presented in vocal score, while all others are reprinted in their full original form. This anthology may be used independently, or along with any introductory text. The publishers have prepared a set of recordings to accompany *The Norton Scores*.

A few words about the highlighting system employed in the full scores: Each system of score is covered with a light gray screen, and the most prominent line in the music at any given point is spotlighted by a white band (see No. 1 in sample on page *x*). In cases where two or more simultaneous lines are equally prominent, they are each highlighted. When a musical line continues from one system or page to the next, the white highlighting band ends with a wedge shape at the right-hand margin, and its continuation begins with a reverse wedge shape (see No. 2 in sample). By following these white bands in sequence through the score, the listener will perceive the notes corresponding to the most audible lines. Naturally, the highlighting will not *always* correspond with the most prominent instruments in a specific recording, for performances differ in their emphasis of particular lines. In such cases, we have highlighted those parts that, in our opinion, *should* emerge most clearly. (There are occasional passages in complex twentieth-century works where no single line represents the musical continuity. In such passages we have drawn the listener's attention to the most audible musical events while endeavoring to keep the highlighting as simple as possible.) To facilitate the following of highlighted scores, a narrow white band running the full width of the page has been placed between systems when there is more than one on a page.

It must be emphasized that we do not seek here to *analyze* melodic structure, contrapuntal texture, or any other aspect of the music. The highlighting may break off before the end of a phrase when the entrance of another part is more audible, and during long-held notes the attention will usually be drawn to more rhythmically active parts. The highlighting technique has been used primarily for instrumental music; in vocal works, the text printed under the music provides a firm guideline for the novice score-reader.

A few suggestions for the use of this anthology may be found useful:

1. The rudiments of musical notation should be introduced with a view to preparing the student to associate audible melodic contours with their written equivalents. It is more important for beginning students to recognize rising and falling lines, and long and short notes, than to identify specific pitches or rhythms. It is helpful to explain the function of a tie, and the layout of a full score.

2. Before listening to a work, it is best for students to familiarize themselves with the names and abbreviations for instruments used in that particular score (a glossary of instrumental names and abbreviations will be found at the conclusion of the book). We have retained the Italian, German, French, and English names used in the scores reproduced in this anthology. This exposure to a wide range of terminology will prepare students for later encounters with scores.

3. Students should be careful to notice whether there is more than one system on a page of score. They should be alerted for tempo changes, repeat signs, and *da capo* indications. Since performances often differ, it is helpful for the instructor to forewarn the class about the specific repeats made or not made in the recordings used for listening.

4. When a piece is very fast or difficult, it is helpful to listen once without a score.

5. It is best to begin with music that is relatively simple to follow: e.g. (in approximate order of difficulty) Handel, *Comfort ye* from *Messiah;* the first and third movements of Mozart's *Eine kleine Nachtmusik;* the Air from Bach's *Suite No. 3 in D major;* and the second movement of Haydn's *Symphony No. 104 in D major (London).*

6. Important thematic material and passages that are difficult to follow should be pointed out in advance and played either on the recording or at the piano. (We have found that rapid sections featuring two simultaneously highlighted instruments sometimes present difficulties for the students—e.g. Beethoven, *Symphony No. 5,* first movement, m. 65 ff.)

We have attempted to keep the highlighted bands simple in shape while showing as much of the essential slurs and dynamic indication as possible. Occasionally, because of the layout of the original score, stray stems and slurs will intrude upon the white area and instrumental directions will be excluded from the highlighting. (Naturally, the beginning of a highlighted area will not always carry a dynamic or similar indication, as the indication may have occurred measures earlier when the instrument in question was not the most prominent.) As students become more experienced in following the scores, they can be encouraged to direct their attention outside the highlighted areas, and with practice should eventually develop the skill to read conventional scores.

I should like to record here my great debt to the late Nathan Broder, who originated the system of highlighting employed here and whose advice and counsel were invaluable. My thanks go also to Mr. David Hamilton, and to Claire Brook and Kathleen Wilson Spillane of W. W. Norton, for many helpful suggestions. I am most grateful to my wife, Anita, who worked with me on every aspect of the book. She is truly the co-editor of this anthology.

How to Follow the Highlighted Scores

1. The most prominent line in the music at any given time is highlighted by a white band.

2. When a musical line continues from one system (group of staffs) or page to the next, the white highlighted band ends with a wedge shape, and its continuation begins with a reverse wedge shape.

3. By following the highlighted bands in sequence through the score, the listener will perceive the notes corresponding to the most audible lines.

4. A narrow white band running the full width of the page separates one system from another when there is more than one on a page. It is very important to be alert for these separating bands.

5. When two or more lines are equally prominent, they are each highlighted. When encountering such passages for the first time, it is sometimes best to focus on only one of the lines.

A Note on Performance Practice

In performances and recordings of earlier music, certain variations from the printed scores will frequently be observed. These are not arbitrary alterations of the music, but are based upon current knowledge concerning the performance practice of the period. In earlier times, the written notes often represented a kind of shorthand, an outline for performers, rather than a set of rigid instructions. The following specific practices may be noted:

1. Ornaments are frequently added to melodic lines, particularly at cadences and in repetitions of musical material.

2. During the Middle Ages and Renaissance, performers were often expected to supply sharps, flats, and naturals that were not written in the music. Some modern editors indicate these accidentals above the notes,

while others do not. Moreover, modern editors and performers often differ in their interpretation of the conventions governing the use of accidentals in early music.

3. In many early sources, the placement of words in relation to notes is not clearly indicated, or shown only in part; thus, modern editions and performances may differ.

4. In music before about 1600, the choice of voices or instruments and the choice of specific instruments was a matter of some freedom. Thus, in performance, some parts of a piece may be played rather than sung, or alternate between voices and instruments.

5. Since, at certain times and places in the past, pitch was higher or lower than it is today, modern performers sometimes transpose music to a key lower or higher than written, in order to avoid performance difficulties.

6. In Baroque music, the figured bass part, consisting of a bass line and numbers indicating harmonies, will be "realized" in different ways by different performers. In some editions included here (e.g. Monteverdi, *L'Orfeo*), a suggested realization is included by the modern editor—but it is only a suggestion, and will not necessarily be followed in a given performance.

THE
NORTON SCORES

An Anthology for Listening

Fourth Edition • Expanded

Volume 1

1. GREGORIAN CHANT, Introit, *Gaudeamus omnes*

In chant notation

AUDE-AMUS omnes in Dó- mi- no

di- em festum ce-le-brántes sub honó- re be- átæ

Ma-rí- æ Vír-gi- nis: de cujus Assumpti-ó- ne

gaudent An- ge- li, et colláu- dant Fí- li- um

De- i.

In modern notation

Gau-de- a - mus om - nes in Do - mi - no, di - em fes - tum

ce - le - bran - tes sub ho-no - re be - a - tae Ma - ri - ae Vir-gi - nis

de cu - jus As-sump-ti - o - ne gau-dent An - ge - li,

et col-lau - dant Fi - li - um De - i.

Translation

Gaudeamus omnes in Domino,
diem festum celebrantes sub honore Mariae
   Virginis:
de cujus Assumptione gaudent Angeli,
et collaudant Filium Dei.

Let us all rejoice in the Lord,
Celebrating a feast-day in honor of the Blessed
   Virgin Mary,
For whose Assumption the angels rejoice
And give praise to the Son of God.

2. GUIRAUT DE BORNELH (c. 1140-1200), *Reis glorios*

Reis glo - ri - os, ve - rais lums e clar - tarz,
Deus po-de-ros, Sen - her, si a vos platz, Al ——— meu com-panh si-atz fi-zels a - ju - da;

Qu'eu no lo vi, —— pos —— la nochs fo, ven-gu - da; Et a-des se-ra—— l'al - ba!

Translation

Reis glorios, verais lums e clartatz,
Deus poderos, Senher, si a vos platz,
Al meu companh siatz fizels a juda;
Qu'eu no lo vi, pos la nochs fo venguda;
    Et ades sera l'alba!

Glorious King, light of truth and splendor
Almighty God, Lord, if it please you,
Give faithful aid to my friend.
I have not seen him since night fell;
    And soon it will be dawn!

Bel companho, si dormetz o veillatz?
Non dormatz plus, suau vos ressidatz,
Qu'en orien vei l'estela creguda
Qu'amean-l jorn, qu'eu l'ai ben coneguda:
    Et ades sera l'alba!

Dear friend, are you asleep or awake?
Sleep no more, now you must rise,
For in the east the star grows bright
That heralds the day. I know it well:
    And soon it will be dawn!

Bel companho, en chantan vos apel:
Non dormatz plus, qu'eu aug chantar l'auzel,
Que vai queren la jorn per lo bocsatge;
Et ai paor que-l gilos vos assatge;
    Et ades sera l'alba!

Dear friend, my song is calling you.
Sleep no more, I hear a bird singing,
He goes seeking daylight through the woods;
I fear the jealous husband will catch you;
    And soon it will be dawn!

The friend replies:

Bel dous companh, tan soi en ric sojorn

Qu'eu no volgra mais fos alba ni jorn.
Car la gensor que anc nasques de naire,
Tenc e abras, per qu'en non prezi gaire
    Lo fol gelos ni l'alba.

My dear sweet friend, I am so happy where
    I am
That I wish for neither dawn nor day.
For the loveliest woman that ever was born
I hold in my arms. So I'm not going to worry
    About the jealous fool or the dawn.

Adapted from Friedrich Gennrich's transcription in *Der Musikalische Nachlass der Troubadours.*

3. ANONYMOUS MOTET, *O miranda dei karitas—Salve mater salutifera—Kyrie* (13TH CENTURY)

The Gregorian chant *Kyrie XII*, cantus firmus for the tenor

Translation

TRIPLUM

O miranda dei karitas!
Per peccatum cecidit
Homo quem condidit
Sed eius bonitas
Relaxavit penas debitas.
Adam mundum perdidit,
Sed vitam reddidit
Christi nativitas.

DUPLUM

Salve, mater salutifera,
Claritatis speculum,
Tu cordis oculum
Nostri considera,
peccatorum sana vulnera.
Virgo, salva seculum
A morte populum
eterna libera.

TENOR

Kyrie

O wondrous love of God!
Through sin fell man
whom he made,
but His goodness
lightened the penalty owed.
Adam destroyed the world,
but life was restored to it
through the birth of Christ.

Hail, healing mother,
mirror of clarity,
consider the eye
of our heart,
heal the sinners' wounds.
Virgin, deliver the world
and free the people
from eternal death.

4. GUILLAUME DE MACHAUT (c. 1300-1377), *Hareu! hareu!—*
Helas! ou sera pris confors—Obediens usque ad mortem

Adapted from Leo Schrade's transcription in *Polyphonic Music of the Fourteenth Century: Guillaume de Machaut.* © Editions de l'Oiseau-Lyre, Les Remparts, Monaco.

spoir que de - vi - ez yert, eins

plus,

Que bonne A-mour de mer - ci l'as - se - u - re

Pour ce que je l'aim plus que nulz,

Par la ver-tu d'es-pe-ran-ce se - u - re.

Et Sou - ve - nir pour en - a - sprir L'ar -

Car pour li seul, qui en-du-re mal meint; Pi - tié def-faut, ou

tou-te biau-té meint; Dur - tés y regne et Dan-giers y re-meint, Des-deins y vit et Loy-au-tez s'i feint

- dour de mon tri - ste de - sir Me moustre a -

Et A-mours n'a de li ne de moy cu - re. Joi-e le het, ma da-me li est du - re,

dés sa grant bon - - té Et

Et, pour croi-stre mes do - le - reus mes-chiés, Met de-dens moy A - mours,

sa fi - ne vrai-e biau - té Qui dou-ble-ment me fait ar - doir.

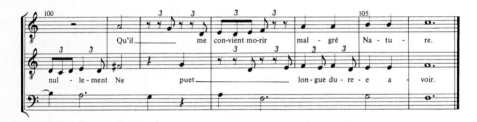

Translation

TRIPLUM

Hareu! hareu! le feu, le feu, le feu	Help! Help! Fire! Fire! Fire!
D'ardant desir, qu'einc si ardant ne fu,	My heart is on fire with burning desire
Qu'en mon cuer a espris et soustenu	Such as was never seen before.
Amours, et s'a la joie retenu	Love, having started it, fans the flames,
D'espoir qui doit attemprer telle ardure.	Withholding all hope of joy which might put out such a blaze.
Las! se le feu qui ensement l'art dure,	Alas, if this fire keeps on burning,
Mes cuers sera tous bruis et esteins,	My heart, already blackened and shriveled,
Qui de ce feu est ja nercis et teins,	Will be burnt to ashes.
Pour ce qu'il est fins, loyaus et certeins;	For it is true, loyal, and sincere.
Si que j'espoir que deviez yert, eins	I expect I shall be mad with grief
Que bonne Amour de merci l'asseure	Before gentle Love consoles it
Par la vertu d'esperance seure.	With sound hope.

Car pour li seul, qui endure mal meint;
Pitié deffaut, ou toute biauté meint;
Durtés y regne et Dangiers y remeint,

Desdeins y vit et Loyautez s'i feint

Et Amours n'a de li ne de moy cure.
Joie le het, ma dame li est dure.

Et, pour croistre mes dolereus meschiés,
Met dedens moy Amours, qui est mes chiés,
Un desespoir qui si mal entechiés,
Est que tous biens a de moy esrachiés,
Et en tous cas mon corps si desnature
Qu'il me convient morir malgré Nature.

It alone, suffering much Hardship,
Is devoid of Pity, abode of all beauty.
Instead, Harshness rules over it and
    Haughtiness flourishes.
Disdain dwells there, while Loyalty is a rare
    visitor
And Love pays no heed to it or to me.
Joy hates it, and my lady is cruel to it.

To complete my sad misfortune,
Love, my sovereign lord,
Fills me with such bitter despair
That I am left penniless,
And so wasted in body
That I shall surely die before my time.

DUPLUM

Helas! ou sera pris confors
Pour moy qui ne vail nés que mors?
Quant riens garentir ne me puet
Fors ma dame chiere qui wet
Qu'en desespoir muire, sans plus,
Pour ce que je l'aim plus que nulz,
Et Souvenir pour enasprir
L'ardour de mon triste desir
Me moustre adés sa grant bonté

Et sa fine vraie biauté
Qui doublement me fait ardoir.
Einssi sans cuer et sans espoir,
Ne puis pas vivre longuement,
N'en feu cuers humeins nullement
Ne puet longue duree avoir.

Alas, where can I find consolation
Who am as good as dead?
When my one salvation
Is my dear lady,
Who gladly lets me die in despair,
Simply because I love her as no other could,
And Memory, in order to keep
My unhappy desire alive,
Reminds me all the while of her great goodness

And her delicate beauty,
Thereby making me want her all the more.
Deprived thus of heart and hope
I cannot live for long.
No man's heart can long survive
When once aflame.

TENOR

Obediens usque ad mortem

Obedient unto death

5. MACHAUT, *Rose, liz, printemps*

Adapted from Leo Schrade's transcription in *Polyphonic Music of the Fourteenth Century: Guillaume de Machaut.* © Editions de l'Oiseau-Lyre, Les Remparts, Monaco.

le,___ pas - - - - - - - - - - ses en dou - cour.
puis___ dire_____ et par hon - nour.

Translation

Rose, liz, printemps, verdure,
Fleur, baume et tres douce odour,
Belle, passes en doucour.

Et tous les biens de Nature,
Avez dont je vous aour.
Rose, liz, printemps, verdure,
Fleur, baume et tres douce odour.

Et quant toute creature
Seurmonte vostre valour,
Bien puis dire et par honnour:

Rose, liz, printemps, verdure,
Fleur, baume et tres douce odour,
Belle, passes en doucour.

Rose, lily, Spring, grass,
Flower, balm, and very sweet odor,
Lovely one, whom you surpass in sweetness.

And all good things of Nature
With which I endow you.
Rose, lily, Spring, grass,
Flower, balm, and very sweet odor.

And if any living thing
Surpass your worth,
Then can I say on my honor:

Rose, lily, Spring, grass,
Flower, balm, and very sweet odor,
Lovely one, whom you surpass in sweetness.

6. GUILLAUME DUFAY (1400-1474),
Alma redemptoris mater (c. 1495)

The chant *Alma redemptoris mater*, on which the top voice is based

to - rum _____ mi - se - re - re.

Translation

Alma redemptoris mater,
quae pervia caeli porta manes,
Et stella maris, succurre cadenti,
surgere qui curat populo.

Tu quae genuisti, natura mirante,
tuum sanctum Genitorem,
Virgo prius ac posterius,
Gabrielis ab ore sumens illud Ave,
peccatorum miserere.

Gracious mother of the Redeemer,
Abiding at the doors of Heaven,
Star of the sea, aid the falling,
Rescue the people who struggle.

Thou who, astonishing nature,
Has borne thy holy Creator,
Virgin before and after,
Who heard the Ave from the mouth of Gabriel,
Be merciful to sinners.

7. DUFAY, *Navré je sui*

Contratenor

Tenor

1.4.7. Nav - ré je sui d'un dart pe - ne - tra - tif Qui m'a per -
3. Tout souel - le - ment, se con - fort n'est ac - tif, En ve - ri -
5. Las, que fe - ray, se dan - gier m'est ac - tif, J'au - ray re -

Navre je sui

Navre je sui

cié le cuer de part en part;
te joy - e de moy de part.
fus con - tre moy, main et tart.

2.8. C'est ma - da - me qui par son doulx re - gart Ai - mab - le me l'a
6. Ne scay qui puist la poin - tu - re du dart En moy ga - rir se

point jus - ques au vif.
non le vray mo - tif.

Translation

Navré je sui d'un dart penetratif Qui m'a percié le cuer de part en part;	I have been wounded by a sharp arrow That has pierced my heart through and through;
C'est ma dame qui par son doulx regart Aimable me l'a point jusques au vif.	It is my lady who with her glance so sweet And dear has stabbed me to the quick.
Tout quellement, se confort n'est actif, En verité joye de moy depart. Navré je sui d'un dart penetratif Qui m'a percié le cuer de part en part.	All alone, if comfort come not soon, In truth all joy will leave me. I have been wounded by a sharp arrow That has pierced my heart through and through.
Las, que feray se dangier m'est actif? J'auray refus contre moy, main et tart, Ne sçay qui puist la pointure du dart En moy garir se non le vray motif.	Alas, what shall I do if the danger is real? That I will be refused, early and late, I know not who can heal me of the wound Except the one who caused it.
Navré je sui d'un dart penetratif Qui m'a percié le cuer de part en part;	I have been wounded by a sharp arrow That has pierced my heart through and through;
C'est ma dame qui par son doulx regart Aimable me l'a point jusques au vif.	It is my lady who with her glance so sweet And dear has stabbed me to the quick.

8. ANONYMOUS, *Saltarello*

Adapted from transcription in *Archiv für Musikwissenschaft*.

9. KONRAD PAUMANN (c. 1410-1473), *Elend, du hast umfangen mich*

From *Geschichte der Musik in Beispielen* by Arnold Schering, used by permission of Breitkopf &
Härtel, Wiesbaden.

10. ANONYMOUS, Basse Danse, *La Spagna* (PUBL. 1494)

11. JOSQUIN DES PREZ (c. 1450-1521), Agnus Dei from *Missa L'Homme armé (sexti toni)* (PUBL. 1502)

The tune *L'homme armé*

L'hom - me, l'hom - me, l'hom - me ar - mé, l'hom - me ar - mé, L'hom - me ar -

mé doibt on dou - ter. On a fait par - tout cri - er

Que chas - cun se vien - gue ar - mer D'un hau - bre - gon de fer.

Superius: A - gnus De -

Altus: A - gnus De - i, a - gnus De -

Tenor: A - gnus De -

Bassus: A - - gnus

- - i. qui tol - lis pec - ca

i, a - gnus De - i, qui tol

- - i. tol - lis

De - i, qui tol - -

Translation

Agnus Dei,	Lamb of God,
qui tollis peccata mundi,	Who takest away the sins of the world,
miserere nobis,	Have mercy upon us,
dona nobis pacem.	Grant us peace

12. CLÉMENT JANEQUIN (c. 1485-1558), *Les Cris de Paris* (1529)

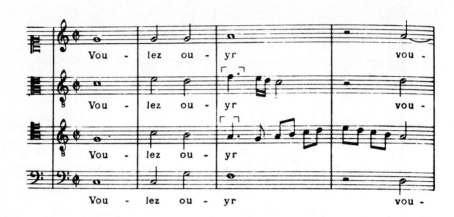

ge - lez, choux ge - lez. Ar - de

choux ge - lez

lez, choux ge - lez choux ge - lez,

nez les ca - mi - na - - - des.

bu - che, bu - - che. Qui veult

choux ge - lez, ge - lez.

choux ge - lez, choux ge - lez. Qui

Choux ge - lez, choux ge - lez.

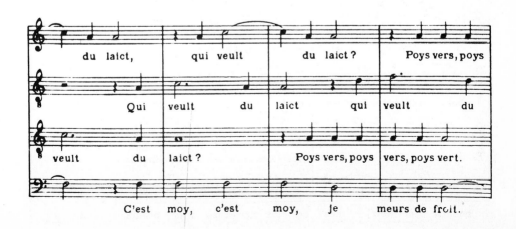

du laict, qui veult du laict? Poys vers, poys

Qui veult du laict qui veult du

veult du laict? Poys vers, poys vers, poys vert.

C'est moy, c'est moy, je meurs de froit.

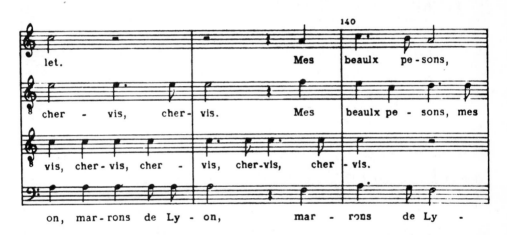
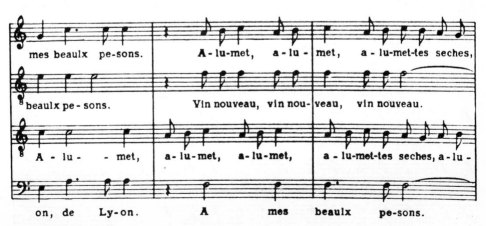

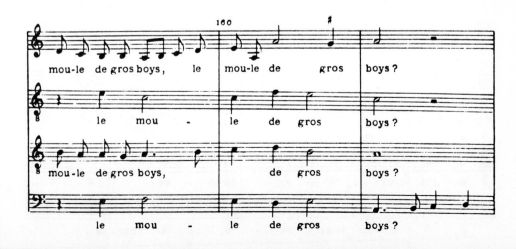

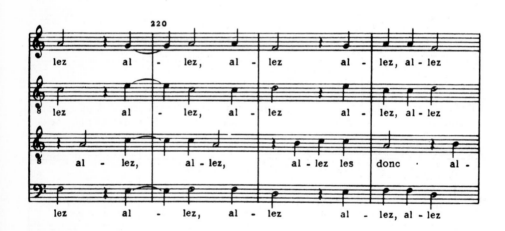

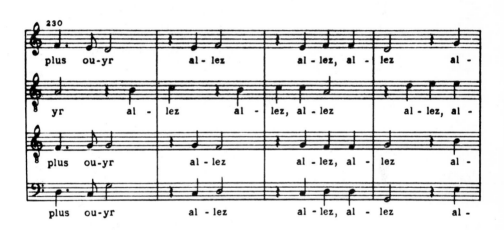

Translation

Voulez ouyr les cris de Paris?	Would you like to hear the cries of Paris?
Où sont ilz ces petiz pions?	Where's the crowd?
Pastez tres tous chaulx, qui l'aira?	The patés are very hot, who will buy them?
Vin blanc, vin cleret, vin vermeil, à six deniers.	White and red wine, claret at six sous.
Casse museaux tous chaulx,	Come and get your hot pies,
Je le vendz, je les donne pour ung petit blanc.	I sell them, I give them for a five-spot.
Tartelettes, friandes à la belle gauffre!	Delicious tarts like waffles,
Et est à l'enseigne du berseau	Fresh from the Sign of the Cradle
Qui est en la rue de la Harpe.	Which is on the Rue de la Harpe.
Sa à boyre, ça!	Who wants a tasty drink?
Aigre, vin aigre!	Vinegar, good and sharp!
Faut il point de saultce vert?	Anybody want green sauce?
Moustarde, moustarde fine!	Mustard, excellent mustard!
Harenc blanc, harenc de la nuyt!	White herring, delicious at night!
Cotrez secz, cotrez! souliers vieux!	Cheap doublets! Old shoes!
Arde buche! Choux gelez!	Chewing tobacco! Cold cabbage!
Hault et bas rammonez les caminades!	Who needs a chimney sweep?
Qui veult du laict?	Anybody want milk?
C'est moy, c'est moy, je meurs de froit.	It's me, it's me, I'm dying of cold!
Poys vers! Mes belles lestues, mes beaulx cibotz!	Green peas! My beautiful lettuce! Onions!
Guigne, doulce guigne!	Cherries, sweet cherries!
Fault il point de sablon? Voire joly!	Anybody need soap? What a beauty!
Argent m'y duit, argent m'y fault.	I have money coming to me! I need it!
Gaigne petit! Lye! Alumet! Houseaux vieux!	Small earnings! Lye! Old boots!
Pruneaux de Saint Julien!	Prunes from St. Julien!
Febves de Maretz, febves! Je fais le coqu, moy!	Beans from Maretz! I make husbands jealous!
Ma belle porée, mon beau persin,	My beautiful leeks, lovely parsley!
Ma belle oseille, mes beaulx espinards!	Beautiful sorrel and spinach!
Peches de Corbeil! Orenge! Pignes vuidez!	Peaches from Corbeil! Oranges! Look at these combs!
Charlote m'amye! Apetit nouveau petit!	Charlotte, my darling! Makes your mouth water!
Amendez vous dames, amendez! Allemande nouvelle!	Make yourselves pretty, ladies! Something new from Germany!
Navetz! Mes beaux balais! Rave doulce, rave!	Turnips! My beautiful barley! Sweet radishes!
Feure, feure Brie! A ung tournoys le chapellet!	Wonderful Brie! Prayer beads, very cheap!
Marons de Lyon! Chervis! Mes beaulx pesons!	Chestnuts from Lyon! Limes! A pair of scales, the best!
Alumet, alumet, alumette seches! Vin nouveau!	Dry tinder wood! New wine!
Fault il point de grois? Choux, petit choux tous chaulx!	Anybody need lard? Sweet hotcakes!

Fault il point de gros boys? Choux gelez!
Et qui l'aura le moule de gros boys?
Eschaudez chaux! Seche bouree!
Serceau beau serseau! Arde chandelle!
    Palourde!
A Paris sur petit point geline de feurre!

Si vous en voulez plus ouyr, allez les donc
    querre!

Anyone for tinder wood? Cold cabbage!
Anybody need a hamper for wood?
Plaster you can heat! Dry firewood!
Hoops, lovely hoops! A candle that burns!
    Cockles!
In Paris they scatter straw over the little
    bridge!
If you want to hear more, go ask them about it!

13. JACOB ARCADELT (c. 1505-c. 1560), *Il bianco cigno* (PUBL. 1539)

In the Recordings for *The Norton Scores*, this is sung a tone higher.

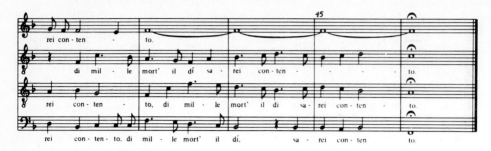

Translation

Il bianco e dolce cigno cantando more,
et io piangendo giung'al fin del viver mio;
stran'e diversa sorte, ch'ei morte sconsolato,
et io moro beato.

Morte che nel morire,
m'empie di gioia tutt'e di desire;
se nel morir'altro dolor non sento,
di mille mort'il di sarei contento.

The sweet white swan dies singing,
While I weep as I reach my life's end.
How strange that he dies disconsolate
And I die happy.

Weary to the point of death,
Drained of all joy and desire,
I meet death without sorrow,
Content to die a thousand deaths a day.

14. GIOVANNI PIERLUIGI DA PALESTRINA (c. 1525-1594),
Sanctus from *Missa Ascendo ad Patrem* (PUBL. 1601)

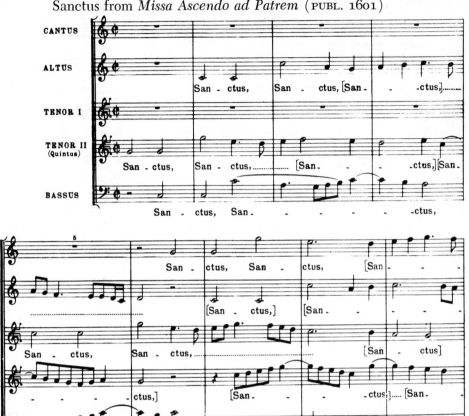

Benedictus

Translation

Sanctus, sanctus, sanctus,
Dominus Deus Sabaoth.
Pleni sunt coeli et terra gloria tua;
Hosanna in excelsis.
Benedictus qui venit in nomine Domini;

Hosanna in excelsis.

Holy, holy, holy,
Lord God of hosts.
Heavens and earth are full of thy glory;
Hosanna in the highest.
Blessed is he that cometh in the name of the
Lord;
Hosanna in the highest.

15. ROLAND DE LASSUS (c. 1532-1594),
Introduction and first motet from *Prophetiae sibyllarum* (c. 1560)

Car - mi - na chro - ma - ti - ca, quae au - dis mo -

Car - mi - na chro - ma - ti - ca, quae au - dis mo -

Car - mi - na chro - ma - ti - ca, quae au - dis mo -

Car - mi - na chro - ma - ti - ca, quae au - dis mo -

du - la - ta te - no - re, Haec sunt il - la,

du - la - ta te - no - re, Haec sunt il - la,

du - la - ta te - no - re, Haec sunt il - la,

du - la - ta te - no - re, Haec sunt il - la, qui -

qui - bus nos - trae o - lim ar - ca - na sa - lu - tis Bis se -

qui - bus nos - trae o - lim ar - ca - na sa - lu - tis Bis se -

qui - bus nos - trae o - lim ar - ca - na sa - lu - tis Bis se -

bus nos - trae o - lim ar - ca - na sa - lu - tis Bis se -

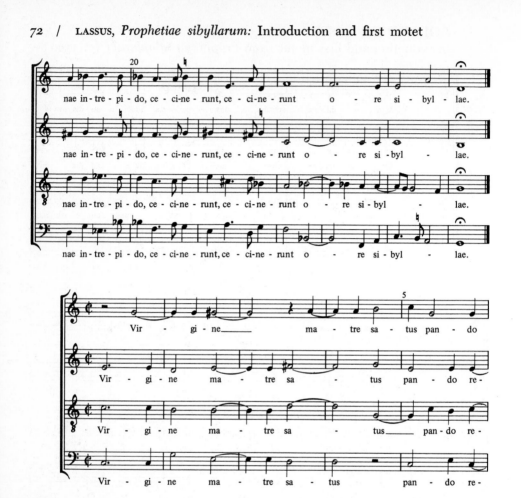

nae in - tre - pi - do, ce - ci-ne - runt, ce - ci-ne - runt o - re si - byl - lae.

nae in - tre - pi - do, ce - ci-ne - runt, ce - ci-ne - runt o - re si - byl - lae.

nae in - tre - pi - do, ce - ci-ne - runt, ce - ci-ne - runt o - re si - byl - lae.

nae in - tre - pi - do, ce - ci-ne - runt, ce - ci-ne - runt o - re si - byl - lae.

Vir - gi - ne____ ma - tre sa - tus pan - do

Vir - gi - ne ma - tre sa - tus pan - do re -

Vir - gi - ne ma - tre sa - tus____ pan - do re -

Vir - gi - ne ma - tre sa - tus pan - do re -

re - si - de - bit a - sel - li, Ju -

si - de - bit a - sel - li, Ju - cun - dus

si - de - bit a - sel - li, Ju - cun - dus prin -

si - de - bit a - sel - li, Jun - cun - dus prin -

Translation

Carmina chromatica,
   quae audis modulata tenore,
Haec sunt illa,
   quibus nostrae olim arcana salutis
Bis senae intrepido,
   cecinerunt ore sibyllae.

SIBYLLA PERSICA
Virgine matre satus pando residebit aselli,

Jucundus princeps unus qui ferre salutem

Rite queat lapsis tamen illis forte diebus.
Multi multa ferent immensi fata laboris,
Solo sed satis est oracula prodere verbo:

Ille Deus casta nascetur virgine magnus.

Chromatic songs,
   which you hear in artful modulation,
These are the ones
   in which the secrets of our salvation
With bold voices, long ago,
   were sung by the twelve sibyls.

PERSIAN SIBYL
Born of a virgin, he will sit on the back of
   an ass.
The joyous prince who alone will bring
   happiness,
He the mighty one, in days to come.
Many will bear the heavy burden of labor,
Yet a single word is enough to utter the
   prophecy:
That great God will be born of a pure virgin.

16. CLAUDIO MONTEVERDI (1567-1643),
Scene from *L'Orfeo* (1ST PERF. 1607)

ORFEO

Tu se' mor - ta, se' mor - ta mia vi - ta ed io re - spi - ro? Tu se' da me par-ti - ta, se' da me par - ti - ta per mai più, mai più non tor - na - re ed io ri - man - go?__ No, no,__ che se i ver-si al-cu - na co - sa pon - no, n'an-drò si-cu - ro a più pro-fon - di a-bis - si,

335

e in - - te - ne - ri - to il cor — del re de l'om - bre, me - co trar - rot - ti

340

a ri - ve - der le stel - le, o se ciò ne - ghe - ram - mi em - pio de - sti - no,

345

ri - mar - rò te - co, in com - pa - gnia di mor - te. Ad - dio ter - ra,

350

ad - dio cie - lo, e so - le, ad - di - - - o.

CORO DI NINFE E PASTORI

Translation

ORFEO

Tu se' morta, se' morta, mia vita,
ed io respiro; tu se' da me partita,
se' da me partita per mai più,
mai più non tornare, ed io rimango—
no, no, che se i versi alcuna cosa ponno
n'andrò sicuro al più profondi abissi,
e intenerito il cor del re dell'ombre,

meco trarotti a riveder le stelle,
o se ciò negherammi empio destino,
rimarrò teco in compagnia di morte!
Addio terra, addio cielo, e sole, addio.

CORO DI NINFE E PASTORI

Ahi, caso acerbo, ahi, fat'empio e crudele,
ahi, stelle ingiuriose, ahi, cielo avaro.
Non si fidi uom mortale di ben caduco e frale,

che tosto fugge, e spesso a gran salita il
precipizio è presso.

You are dead, dead, my darling,
And I live; you have left me,
Left me forevermore,
Never to return, yet I remain—
No, no, if verses have any power,
I shall go boldly to the deepest abysses,
And having softened the heart of the king of
shadows,

Will take you with me to see again the stars,
Or if cruel fate will deny me this,
I will remain with you in the presence of death!
Farewell earth, farewell sky, and sun, farewell.

CHORUS OF NYMPHS AND SHEPHERDS

Ah, bitter chance, ah, fate wicked and cruel,
Ah, stars of ill omen, ah, heaven avaricious.
Let not mortal man trust good, short-lived and
frail,

Which soon disappears, for often to a bold
ascent the precipice is near.

17. MONTEVERDI, *Zefiro torna* (PUBL. 1632)

Translation

Zefiro torna e di soavi accenti
L'aer fa grato e'l piè discioglie a l'onde,
E mormorando tra le verdi fronde,
Fa danzar al bel suon su'l prato i fiori;

Inghirlandato il crin Fillide e Clori,
Note temprando amor care e gioconde;
E da monti e da valli ime e profonde,
Raddoppian l'armonia gli antri canori.

Sorge più vaga in ciel l'aurora el Sole,
Sparge più luci d'or più puro argento,
Fregia di Teti più il bel ceruleo manto.

Sol io per selve abbandonate e sole,
L'ardor di due begli occhi el mio tormento,
Come vuol mia ventura hor piango, hor canto.

The West Wind returns and with gentle accents
Makes the air pleasant and quickens one's step,
And, murmuring among the green branches,
Makes the meadow flowers dance to its lovely
    sound.

With garlands in their hair Phyllis and Clorinda
Are sweet and joyous while Love makes music,
And from the mountains and valleys hidden
    deep,
The echoing caves redouble the harmony.

At dawn the sun rises in the sky more gracefully,
Spreads abroad more golden rays, a purer silver,
Adorns the sea with an even lovelier blue mantle.

Only I am abandoned and alone in the forest,
The ardor of two beautiful eyes is my torment:
As my fate may decree, now I weep, now I sing.

18. THOMAS WEELKES (c. 1575-1623),
As Vesta Was Descending (PUBL. 1601)

Long live fair O - ri - a - - - na.

-a - na, Long live fair O - ri - a - na.

live fair O - ri - a - na, fair O - ri - a - na.

-na, fair O - ri a - na.

-na, Long live fair O - ri - a - - na.

O - - - ri - a - - na.

19. HENRY PURCELL (c. 1659-1695),
Dido's Lament from *Dido and Aeneas* (1ST PERF. 1689)

Thy hand, Bel-in-da! dark — — ness shades me, On thy

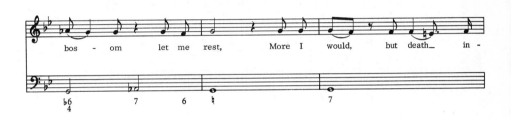

bos-om let me rest, More I would, but death — in-

vades me Death is now — a wel-come guest!

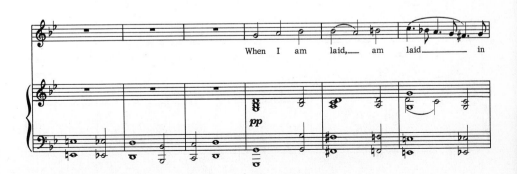

When I am laid, — am laid — in

earth, may my wrongs cre - ate no trou - ble, no trou - ble in___ thy breast.

When I am laid,___ am laid_____ in earth, may my wrongs cre-

ate no trou - ble, no trou - ble in___ thy breast. Re - mem - ber me,

re - mem - ber me, But ah!_____ for - get my fate, Re -

20. ANTONIO VIVALDI (1678-1741), *La Primavera* from *The Four Seasons* (c. 1725)

I

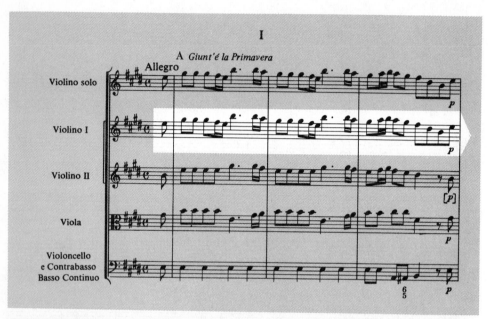

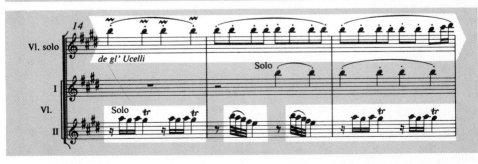

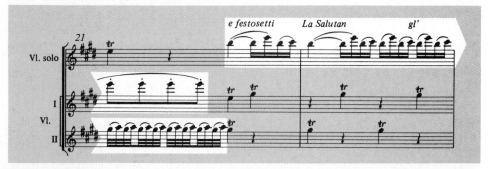

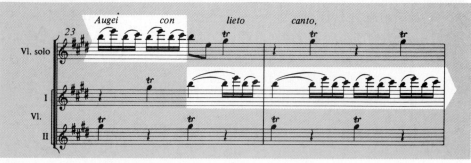

C *Ei fonti allo Spirar de' Zeffiretti Con dolce mormoria*

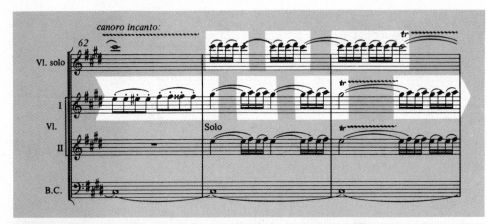

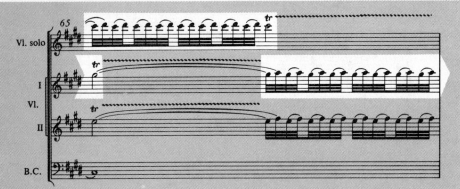

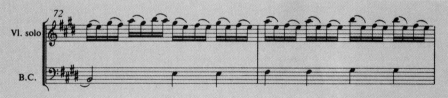

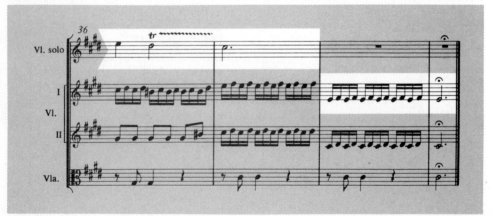

III

DANZA PASTORALE

G *Di pastoral Zampogna al Suon festante Danzan Ninfe e Pastor nel tetto amato*

Di primavera all' apparir brillante.

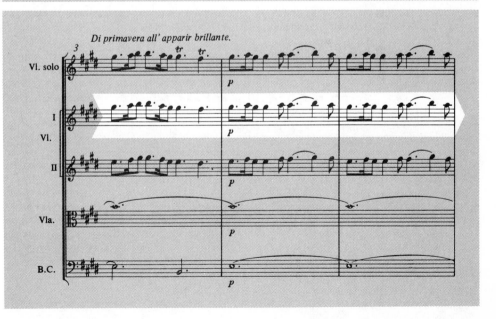

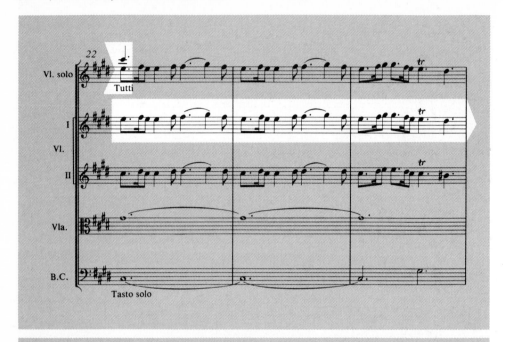

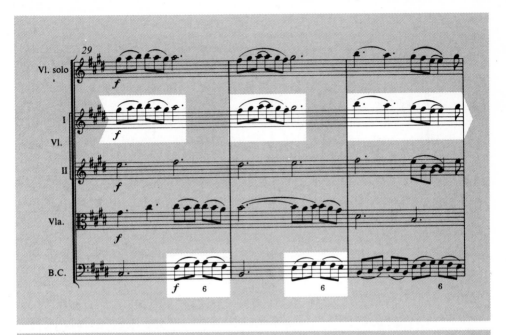

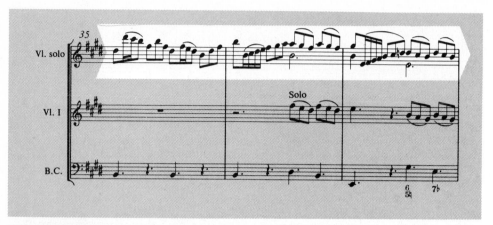

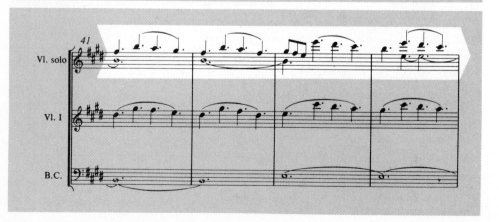

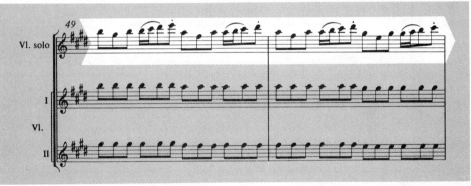

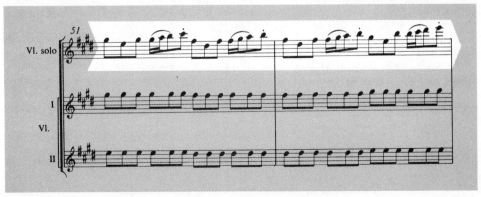

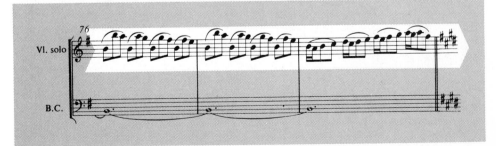

Translation

A Giunt è la Primavera e festosetti
B La salutan gl'Augei con lieto canto,

Spring is here and
the birds greet it festively with their joyous song.

C E i fonti allo spirar de' Zeffiretti
Con dolce mormorio scorrono intanto:

Meanwhile the streams and springs at the breath of gentle breezes run their course with a sweet murmur.

D Vengon' coprendo l'aer di nero amanto
E Lampi, e tuoni ad annuntiarla eletti

Thunder and lightning come to announce the season,
covering the air with a black mantle.

E Indì tacendo questi, gl'Augelletti;
Tornan' di nuovo allor canoro incanto:

When things have quieted down, the little birds return to their melodious warbling.

F E quindi sul fiorito ameno prato
Al caro mormorio di fronde e piante
Dorme'l Caprar col fido can' à lato.

On a pleasant field of flowers, the goatherd sleeps, lulled by the sweet murmur of leaves and plants, his faithful dog by his side.

G Di pastoral Zampogna al Suon festante
Danzan Ninfe e Pastor nel tetto amato
Di primavera all'apparir brillante.

To the gay sounds of bagpipes, nymphs and shepherds dance in the fields resplendent with spring.

21. GEORGE FRIDERIC HANDEL (1685-1759), *V'adoro* from *Giulio Cesare* (1ST PERF. 1724)

gra _ te nel sen, _____ v'a _ do _ ro, pu _ pil _ le, sa _ et _ te d'A _ mo _ re, le vo _ stre fa _

_ vil _ le son _ gra _ te nel sen, _____ le vo _ stre fa _ vil _ le son gra _ te _ nel sen.

Translation

V'adoro, pupille, saette d'amore,   I adore you, O eyes, arrows of love,
le vostre faville son grate nel sen.   Your sparks are pleasing to my heart.
Pietose vi brama il mesto mio core,   My sad heart begs for your mercy,
ch'ogn'ora vi chiama l'amato suo ben.   Never ceasing to call you its beloved.

22. HANDEL, Excerpts from *Messiah* (1741)

No. 1: Overture

No. 2: *Comfort ye*

No. 3: *Ev'ry valley*

No. 4: *And the glory of the Lord*

*) According to the original score.

No. 12: *For unto us a Child is born*

No. 44: *Hallelujah*

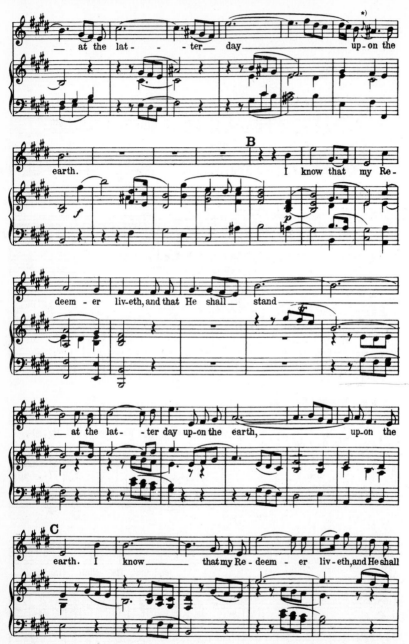

*) This appeggiatura is not in Händel's score

23. JOHANN SEBASTIAN BACH (1685-1750),
Organ Fugue in G minor (Little) (1709?)

24. BACH, *Brandenburg Concerto No. 2 in F major* (1721?)

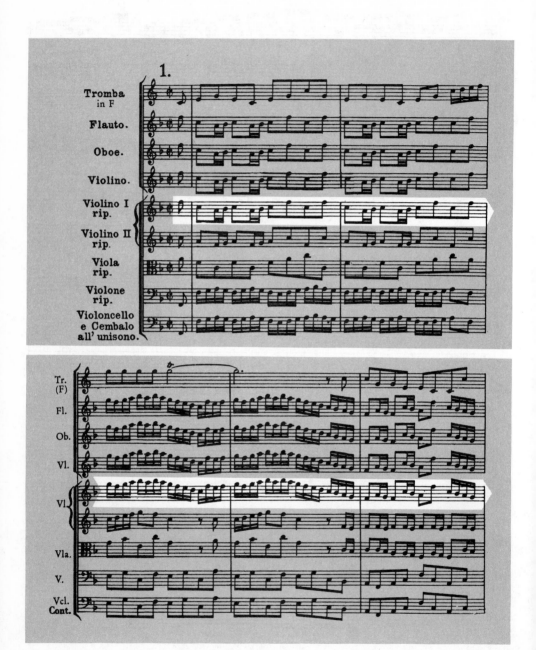

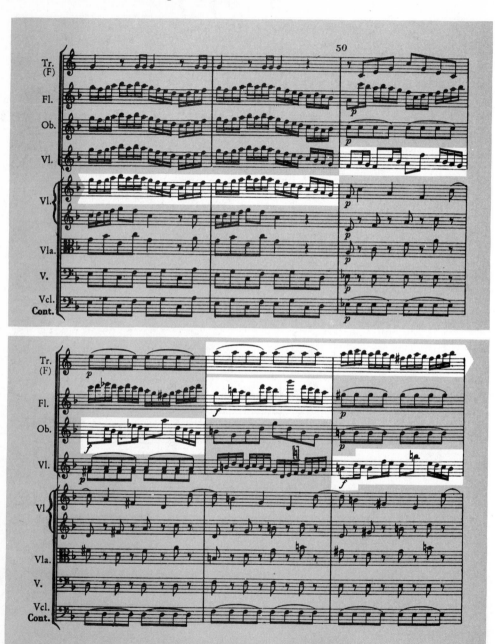

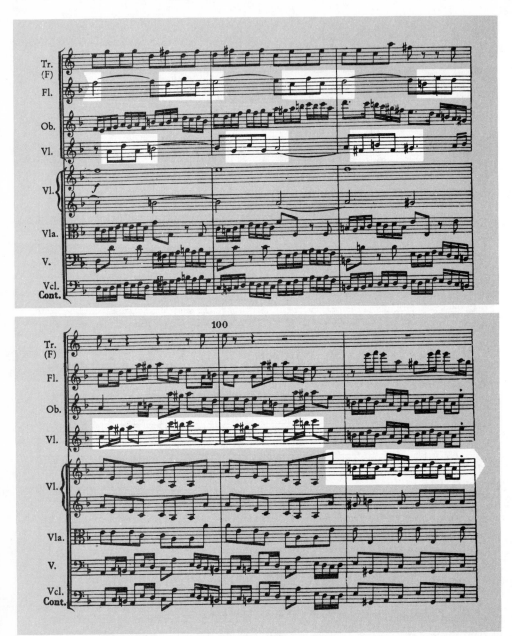

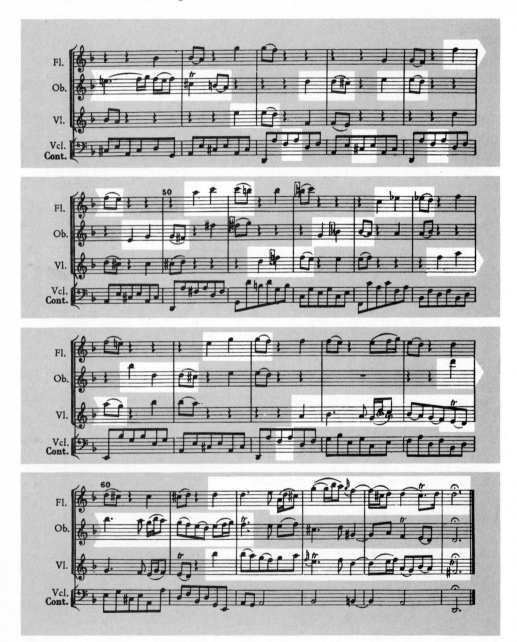

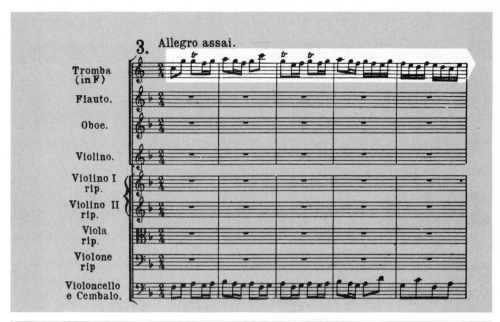

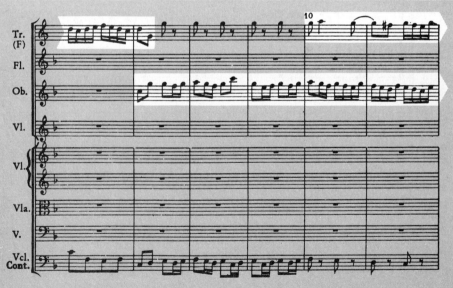

25. BACH, Air and Gigue from *Suite No. 3 in D major* (1723?)

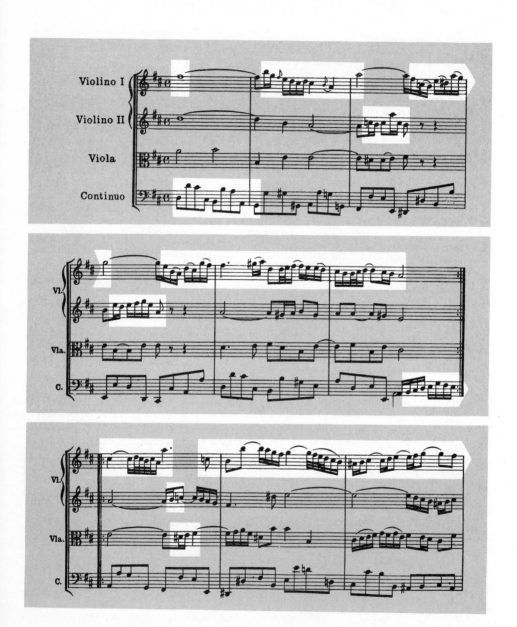

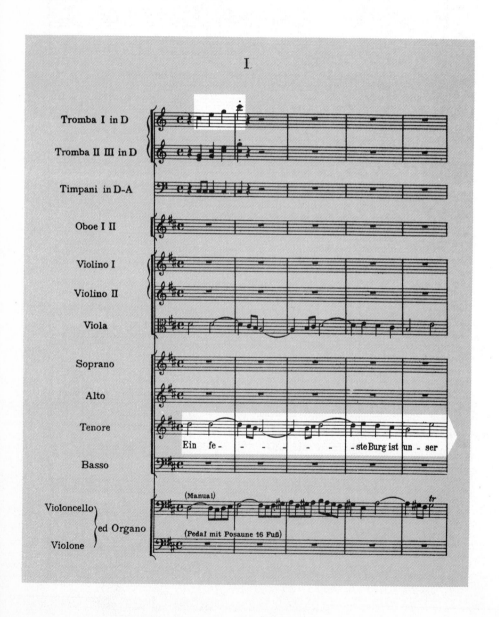

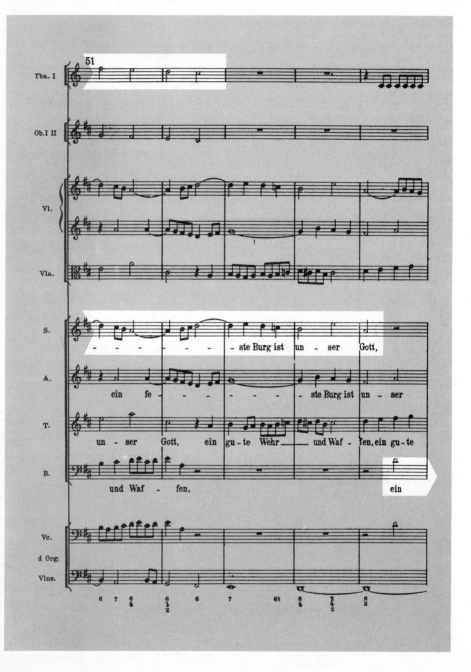

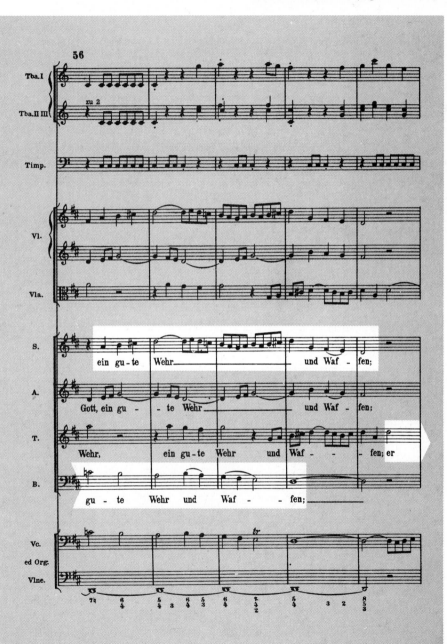

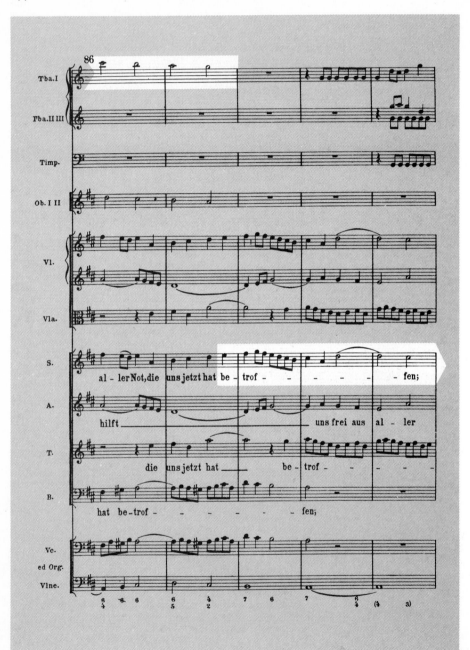

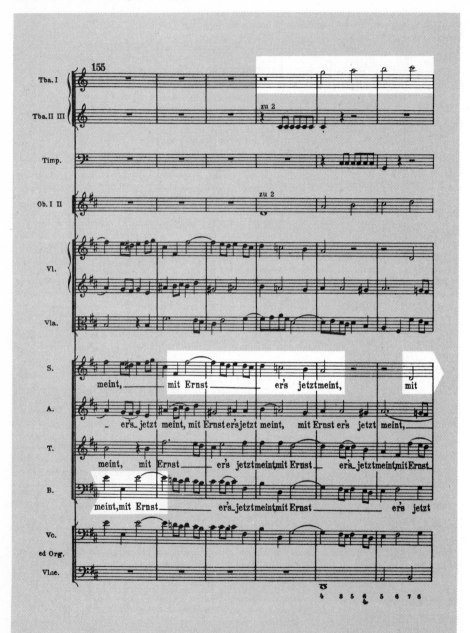

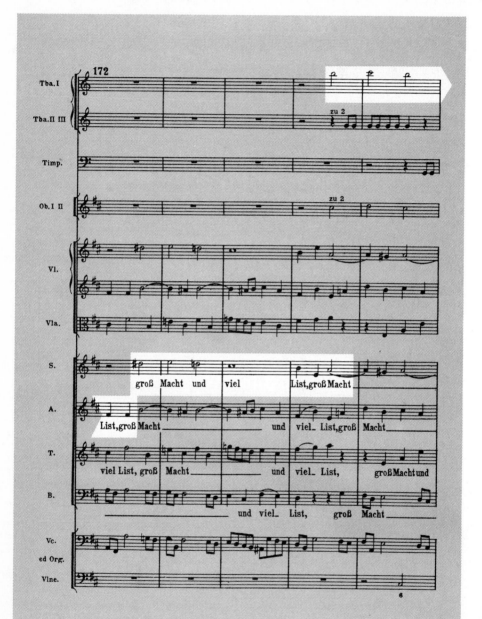

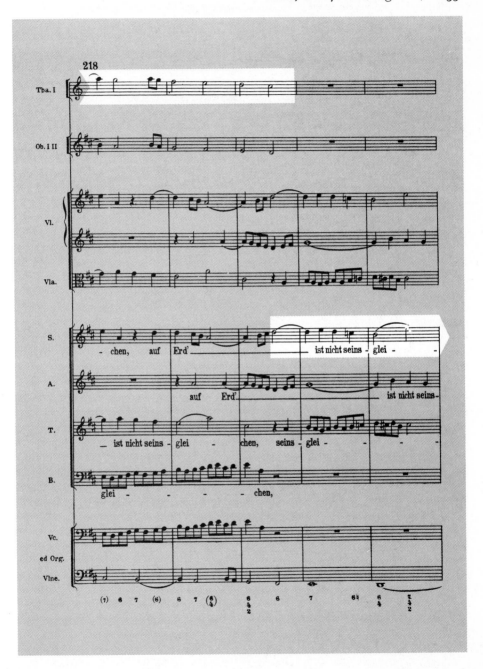

II

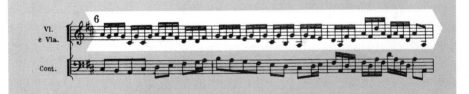

III

Er-wä-ge doch, Kind Got-tes, die so gro-ße Lie-be, da

Je-sus sich mit sei-nem Blu-te dir ver-schrie-be, wo-

mit er dich zum Krie-ge wi-der Sa-tans Heer und wi-der Welt und Sün-de ge-

wor-ben hat. Gib nicht in dei-ner See-le dem

Sa-tan und den La-stern statt! Laß nicht dein Herz, den Him-mel Got-tes auf der

IV

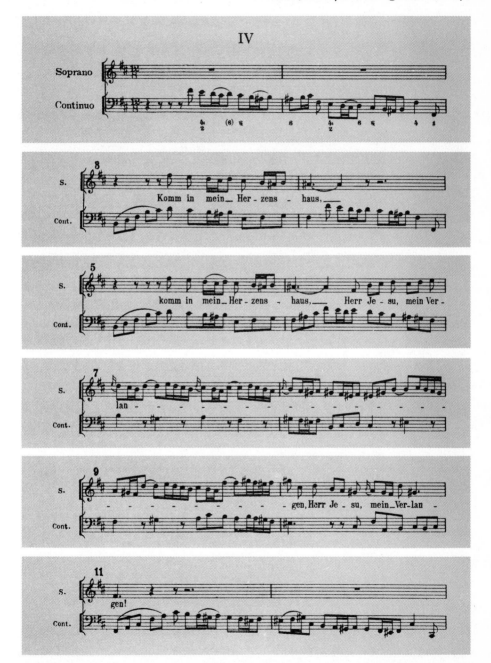

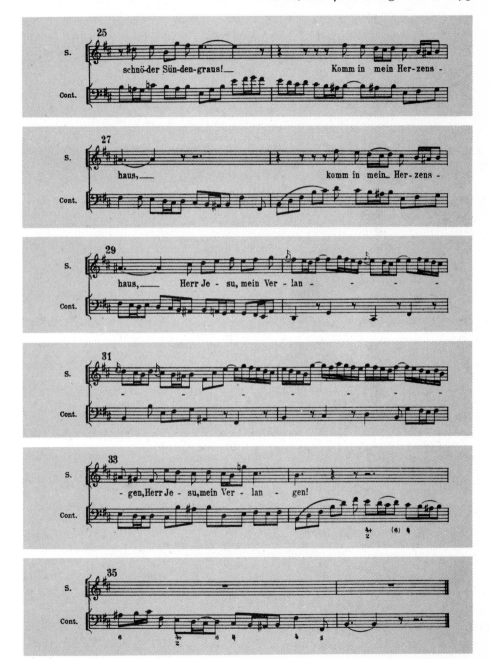

V

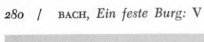

es soll uns doch ge - lin -

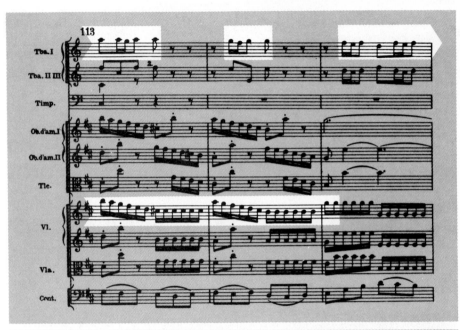

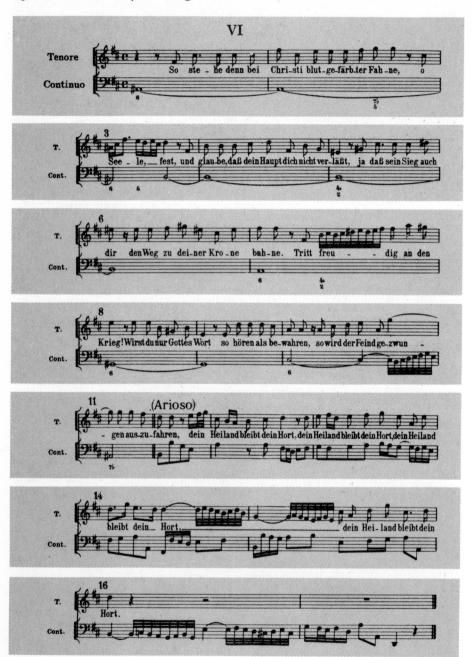

VII

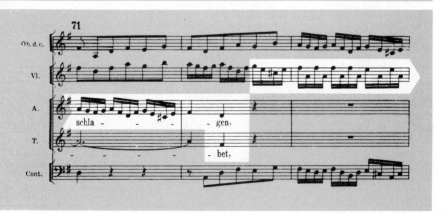

VIII

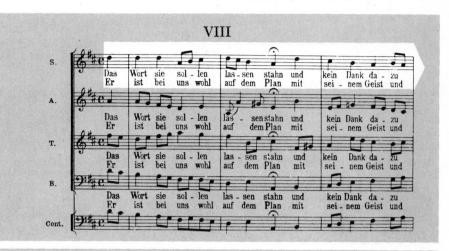

Translation

I

Ein fest Burg ist unser Gott,
  ein' gute Wehr und Waffen;
er hilft uns frei aus aller Not,
die uns jetzt hat betroffen.

    A mighty fortress is our God,
      A good defense and weapon;
    He helps free us from all the troubles
    That have now befallen us.

Der alte böse Feind,
mit Ernst er's jetzt meint,
  gross Macht und viel List
  sein grausam Rüstung ist,
auf Erd' ist nicht seinsgleichen.

    Our ever evil foe;
    In earnest plots against us,
      With great strength and cunning
      He prepares his dreadful plans.
    Earth holds none like him.

II

Mit unsrer Macht ist nichts getan,
  wir sind gar bald verloren.
Es streit't für uns der rechte Mann,
  den Gott selbst hat erkoren.

    With our own strength nothing is achieved,
      We would soon be lost.
    But in our behalf strives the Mighty One,
      whom God himself has chosen.

Fragst du, wer er ist?
Er heisst Jesus Christ,
  der Herre Zebaoth,
  und ist kein andrer Gott,
das Feld muss er behalten.

    Ask you, who is he?
    He is called Jesus Christ,
      Lord of Hosts,
    And there is no other God,
      He must remain master of the field.

Alles was von Gott geboren,
ist zum Siegen auserkoren,
  Wer bei Christi Blutpanier
in der Taufe Treu' geschworen,
  siegt im Geiste für und für.

    Everything born of God
      has been chosen for victory.
      He who holds to Christ's banner,
    Truly sworn in baptism,
      His spirit will conquer for ever and ever.

III

Erwäge doch, Kind Gottes,
  die so grosse Liebe,
da Jesus sich mit seinem Blute
  dir verschriebe,

    Consider, child of God,
      the great love
    That Jesus with his sacrifice
      showed you,

womit er dich zum Kriege
  wider Satan's Heer, und wider Welt
und Sünde geworben hat.
Gib nicht in deiner Seele
  dem Satan und den Lastern statt!

    Whereby he enlisted you
      in the fight against Satan's horde
      and the sinful world.
    Yield no place in your soul
      to Satan and wickedness!

Lass nicht dein Herz,
  den Himmel Gottes auf der Erden,
zur Wuste werden,
  bereue deine Schuld mit Schmerz,

    Do not let your heart,
      God's heaven on earth,
    Become a wasteland,
      repent of your sin with tears,

dass Christi Geist
  mit dir sich fest verbinde.

So that Christ's spirit
  may be firmly united with you.

IV

SOPRANO

Komm in mein Herzenshaus,
  Herr Jesu, mein Verlangen.
Treib Welt und Satan aus,
  und lass dein Bild in mir
erneuert prangen.
Weg, schnöder Sündengraus!

Come dwell within my heart,
  Lord Jesu of my desiring.
Drive out the evil of the world,
  and let Thine image shine before me
in renewed splendor.
Begone, base shape of sin.

V

CHORUS

Und wenn die Welt voll Teufel wär
  und wollten uns verschlingen,
so fürchten wir uns nicht so sehr,
  es soll uns doch gelingen.

Though the world were full of devils
  eager to devour us,
We need have no fear,
  as we will still prevail.

Der Fürst dieser Welt
wie saur er sich stellt,
  tut er uns doch nichts,
  das macht, er ist gericht't,
ein Wörtlein kann ihm fällen.

The Arch-fiend of this world,
No matter how bitter his stand,
  cannot harm us,
  Indeed he faces judgment,
One Word from God will bring him low.

VI

TENOR

So stehe denn bei Christi
  blutgefärbter Fahne, O Seele, fest
und glaube dass dein Haupt
  dich nicht verlässt,
ja, dass sein Sieg auch dir
den Weg zu deiner Krone bahne.

So take your stand firmly
  by Christ's bloodstained banner, O my soul,
And believe that God
  will not forsake you.
Yea, that His victory will lead you too
On the path to salvation.

Tritt freudig an den Krieg!
Wirst du nur Gottes Wort
so hören als bewahren,
so wird der Feind gezwungen auszufahren,
dein Heiland bleibt dein Heil,
dein Heiland bleibt dein Hort.

Go forth joyfully to do battle!
If you but hear God's word
  and obey it,
The Foe will be forced to yield.
Your Savior remains your salvation,
Your Savior remains your refuge.

VII

ALTO AND TENOR

Wie selig sind doch die,

How blessed are they
  whose words praise God,

doch selger ist das Herz,
  das ihn im Glauben trägt.
Es bleibet unbesiegt
  und kann die Feinde schlagen
und wird zuletzt gekrönt,
  wenn es den Tod erlegt.

Yet more blessed is he
  who bears Him in his heart.
He remains unvanquished
  and can defeat his foes,
And is finally crowned
  when Death comes to fetch him.

VIII

CHORUS

Das Wort, sie sollen lassen stahn
  und kein Dank dazu haben.
Er ist bei uns wohl auf dem Plan
  mit seinem Geist und Gaben.

Nehmen sie uns den Leib,
Gut, Ehr, Kind und Weib,
  lass fahren dahin,
  sie habens kein Gewinn;
das Reich muss uns doch bleiben.

Now let the Word of God abide
  without further thought.
He is firmly on our side
  with His spirit and strength.

Though they deprive us of life,
Wealth, honor, child and wife,
  we will not complain,
  It will avail them nothing;
For God's kingdom must prevail.

MOVEMENTS I, II, V, AND VIII BY MARTIN LUTHER
MOVEMENTS III, IV, VI, AND VII BY SALOMO FRANCK

27. DOMENICO SCARLATTI (1685-1757), *Sonata in E major,* K. 46 (PUBL. 1739)

CHRISTOPH WILLIBALD GLUCK (1714-1787),
Che farò senza Euridice? from *Orfeo ed Euridice* (1762, rev. 1774)

29. JOSEPH HAYDN (1732-1809), *Symphony No. 104 in D major (London)* (1795)

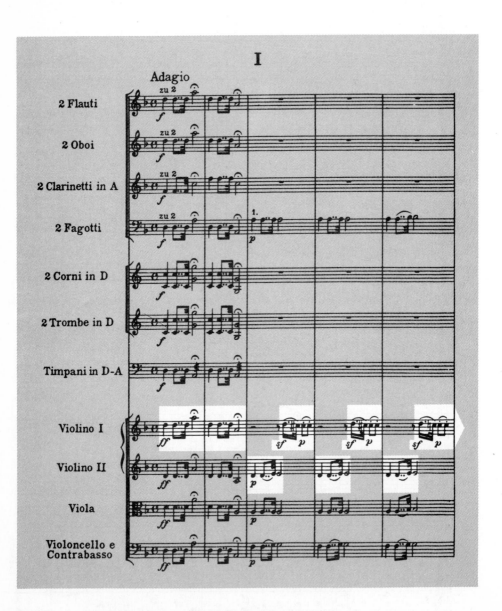

II

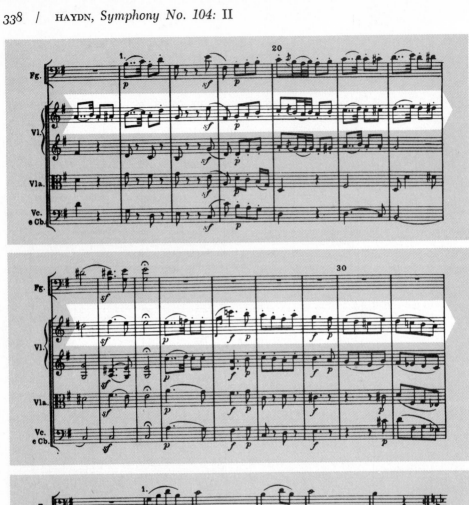

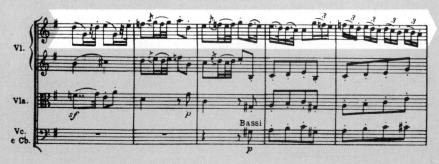

III

Menuetto Allegro

Men. D.C.

IV

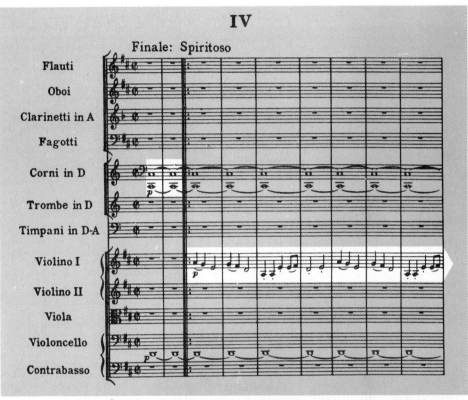

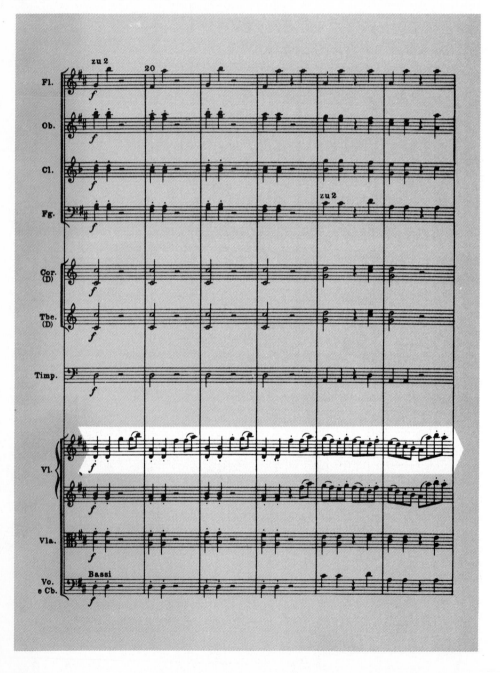

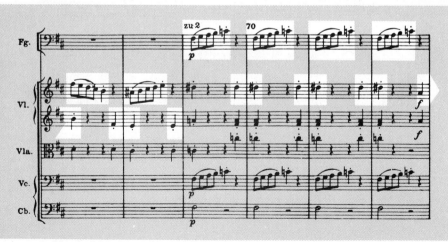

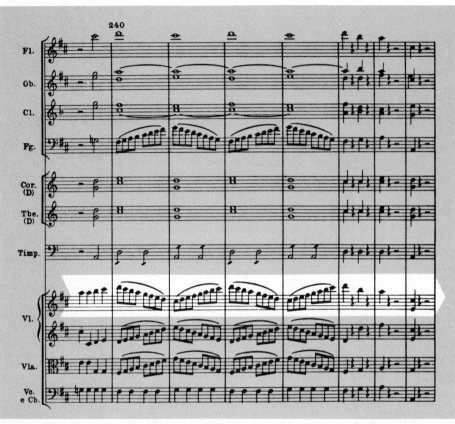

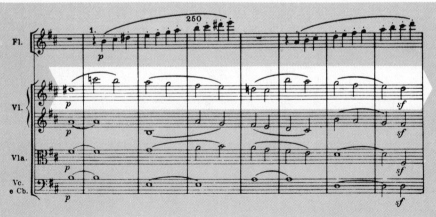

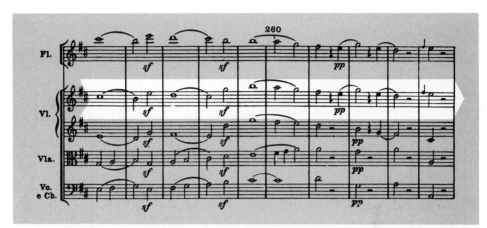

30. WOLFGANG AMADEUS MOZART (1756-1791),
Piano Concerto in C major, K. 467 (1785)

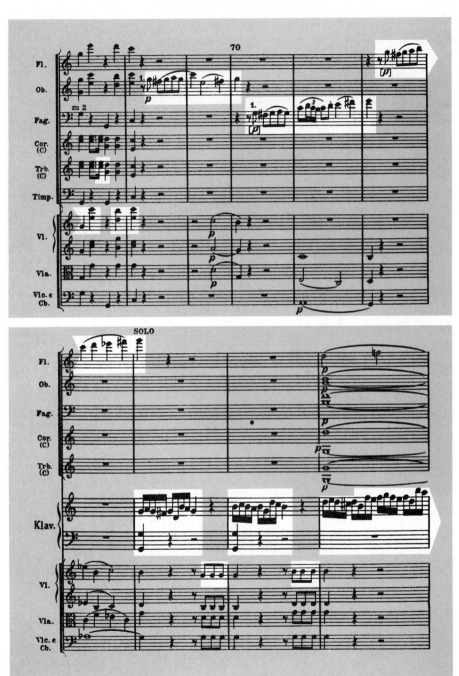

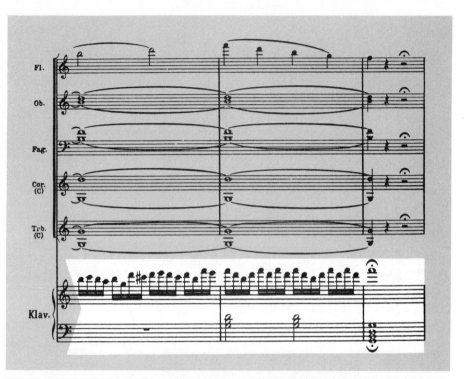

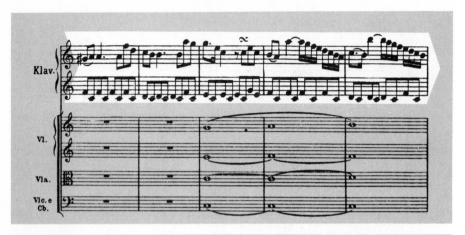

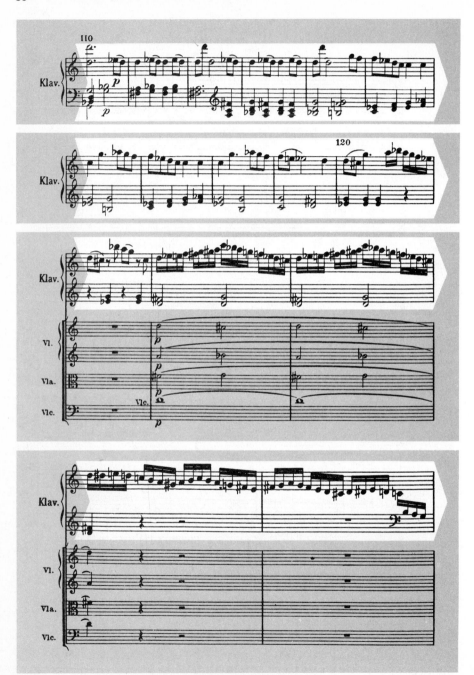

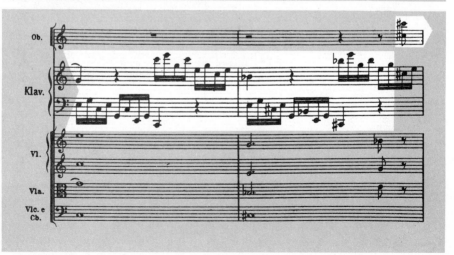

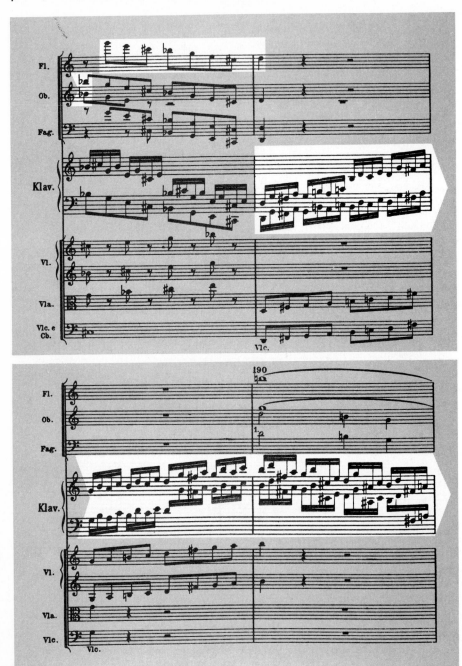

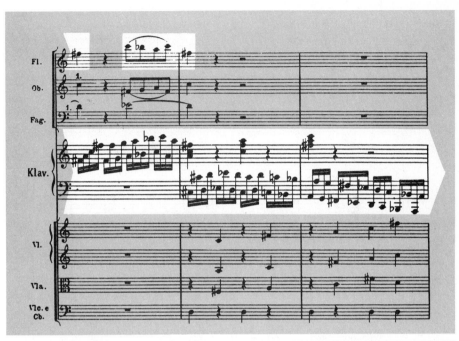

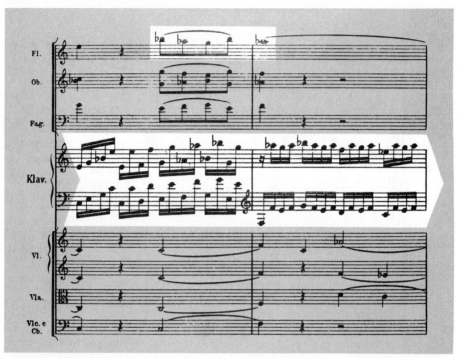

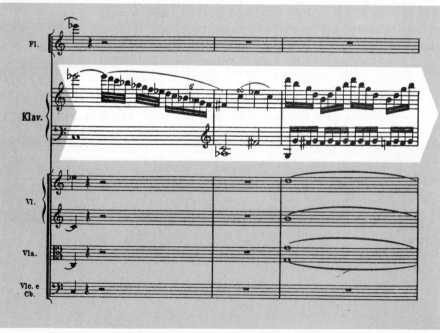

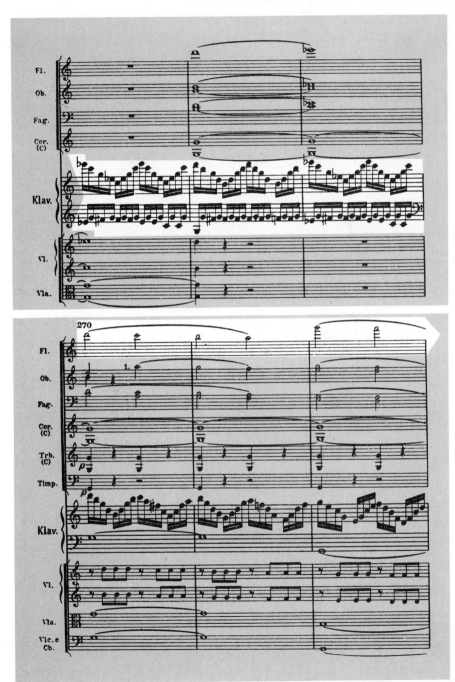

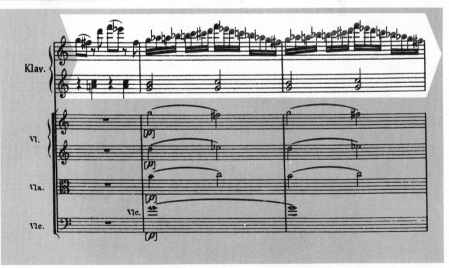

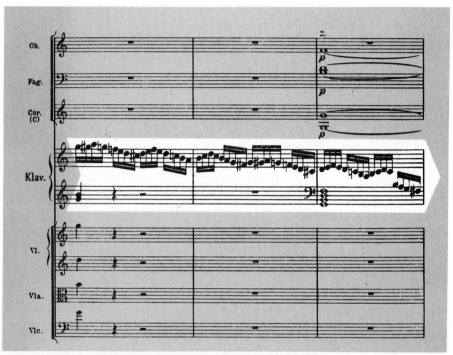

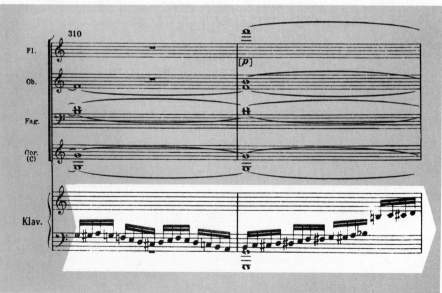

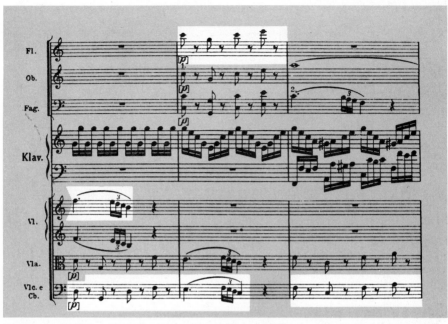

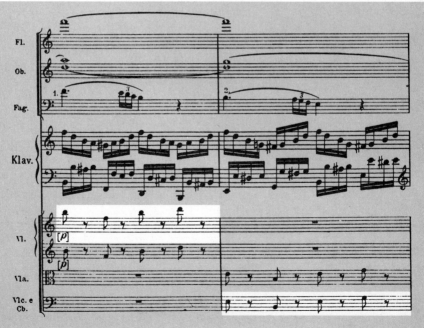

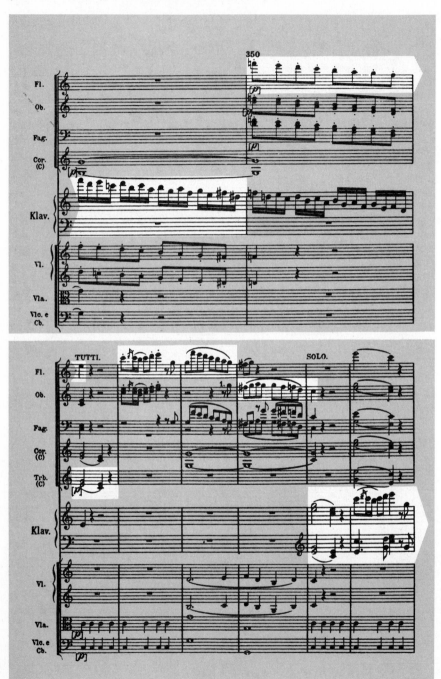

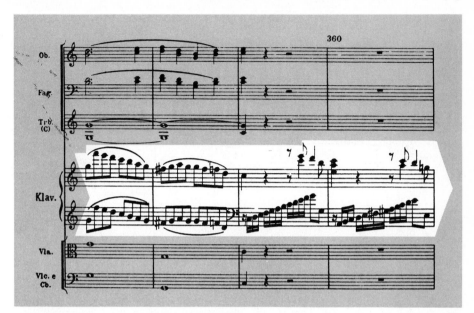

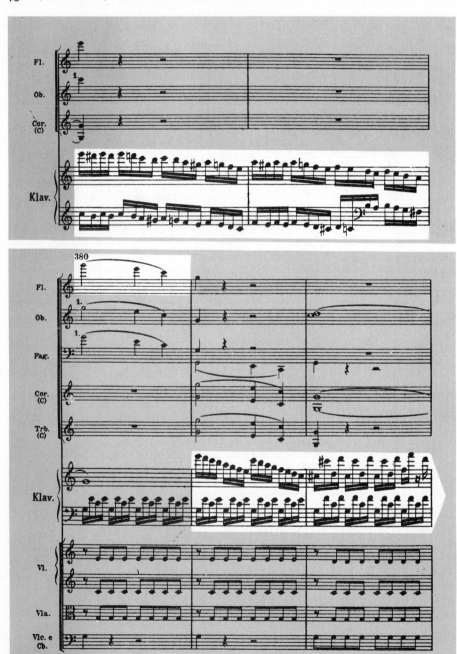

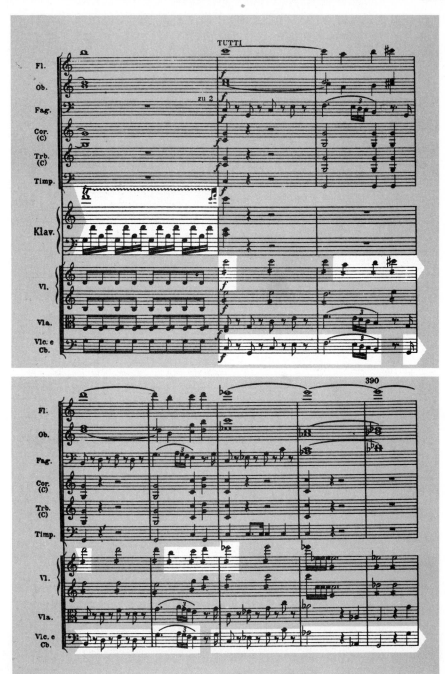

° Mozart did not leave written-out cadenzas for this concerto. Modern pianists supply their own or choose from among various published cadenzas.

II.

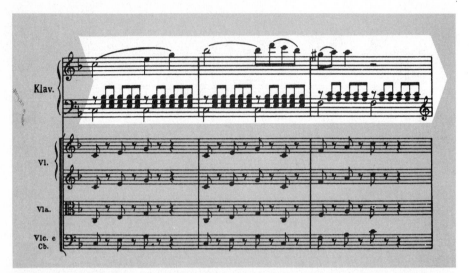

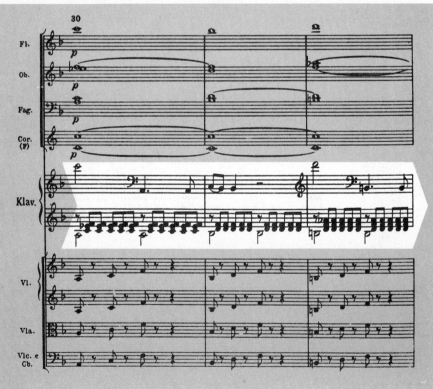

III.

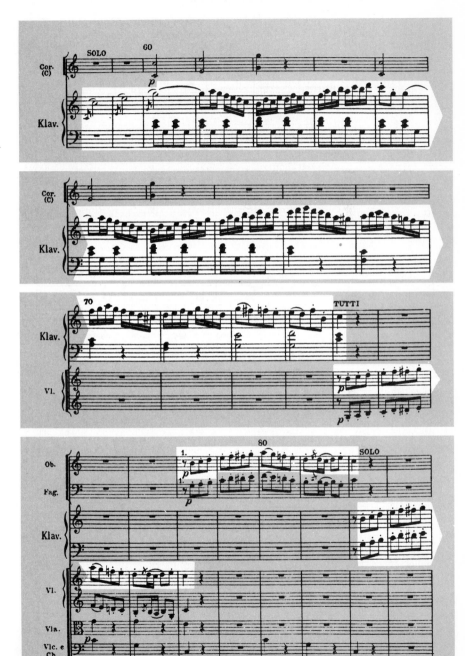

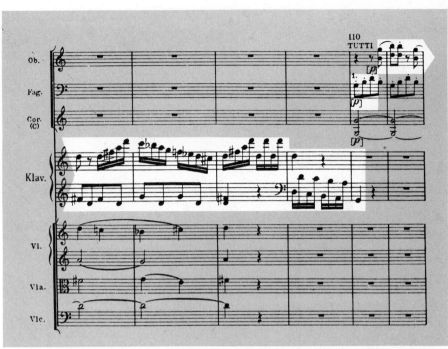

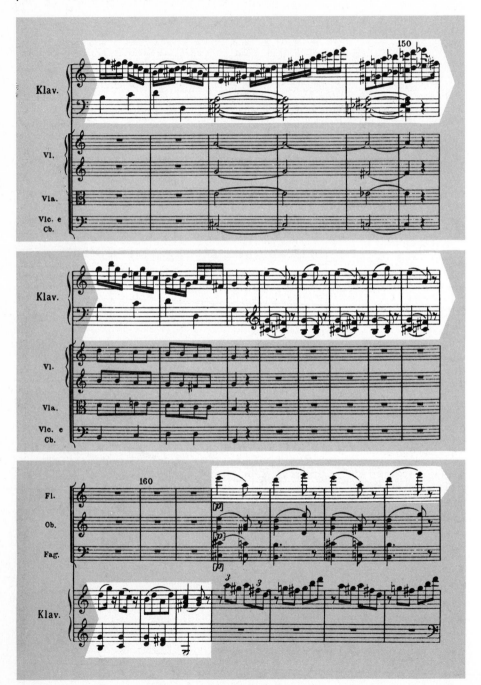

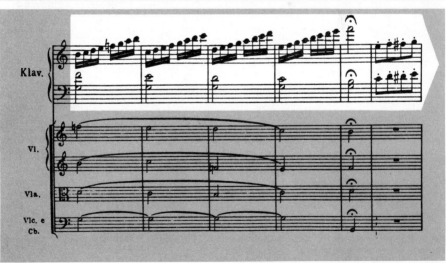

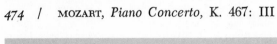

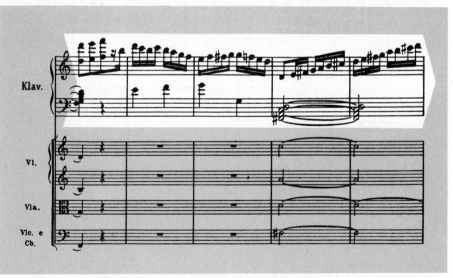

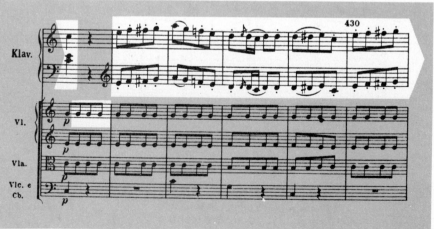

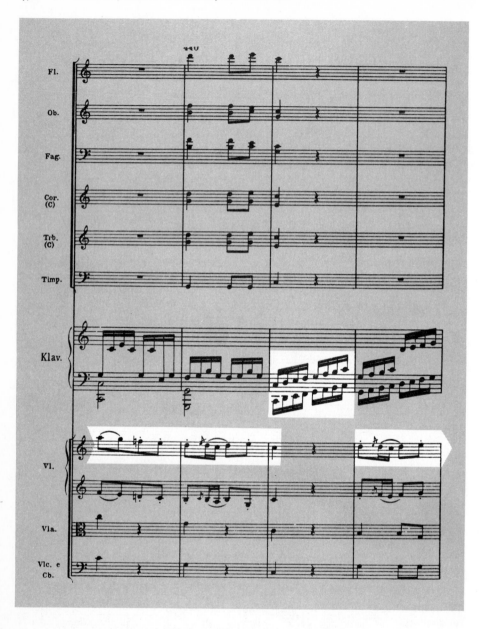

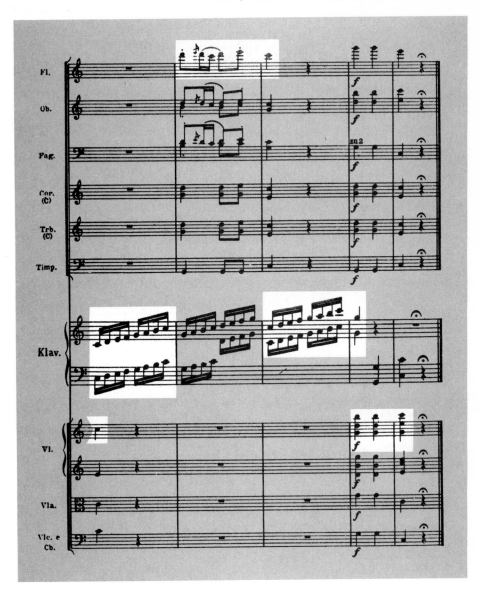

31. MOZART, *Eine kleine Nachtmusik* (1787)

I

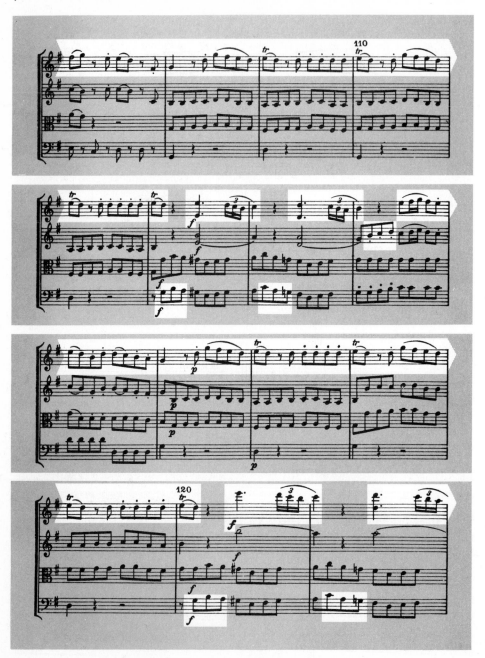

II

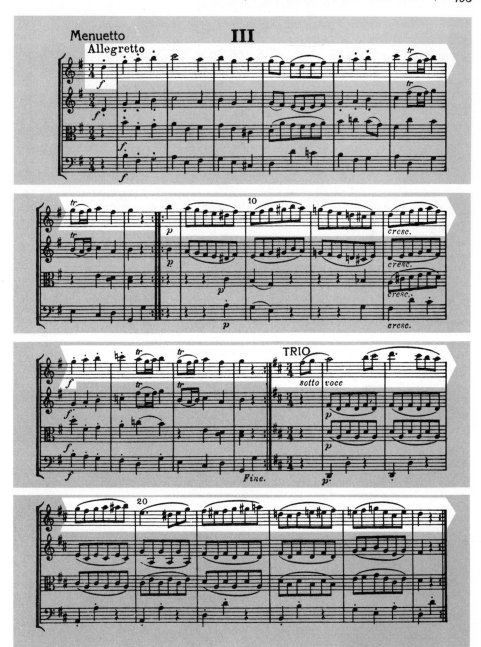

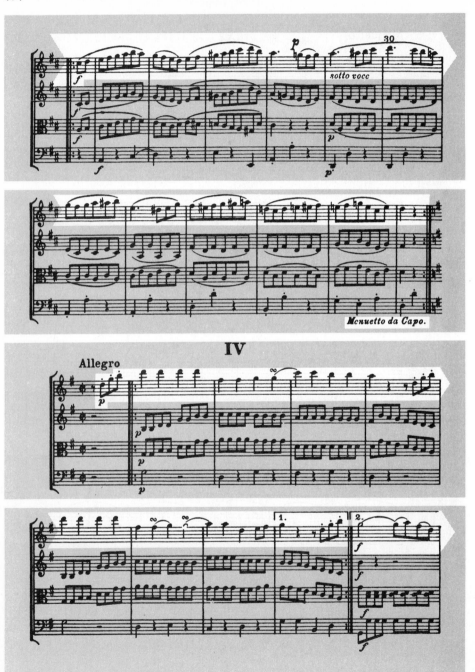

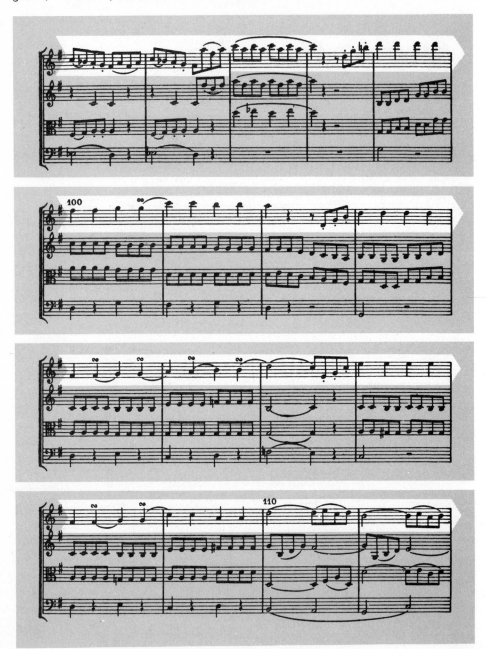

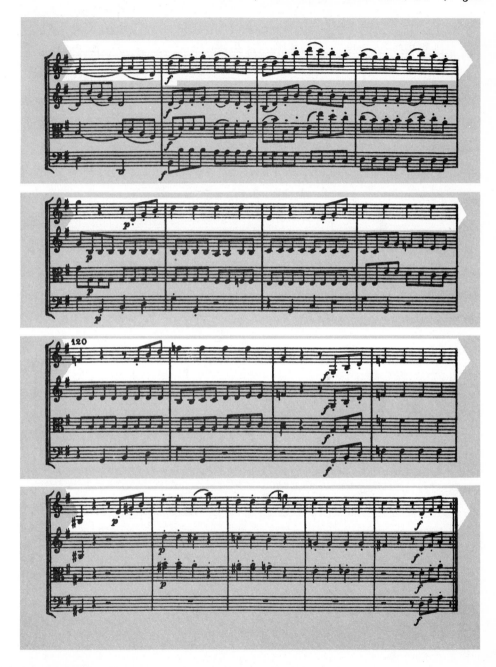

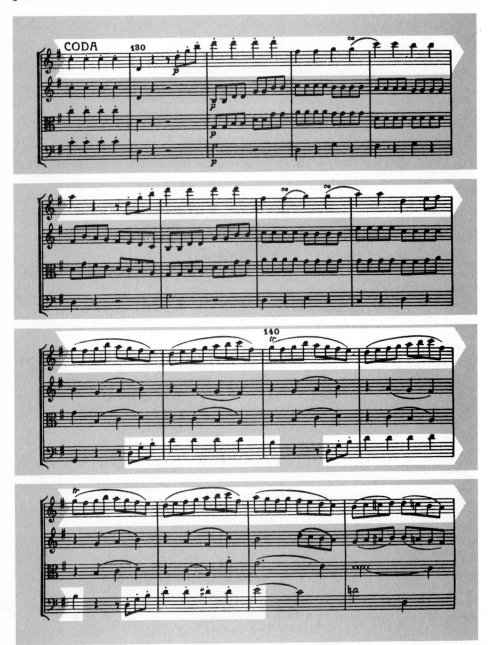

32. MOZART, Excerpts from *Don Giovanni* (1787)
Overture

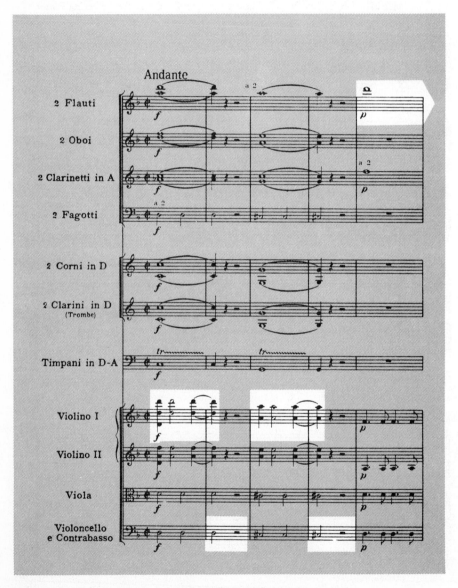

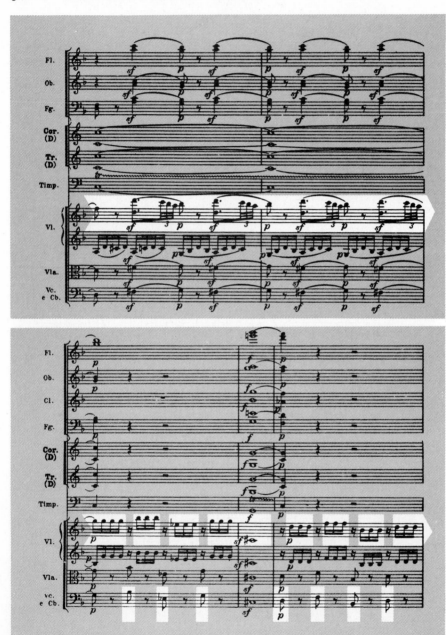

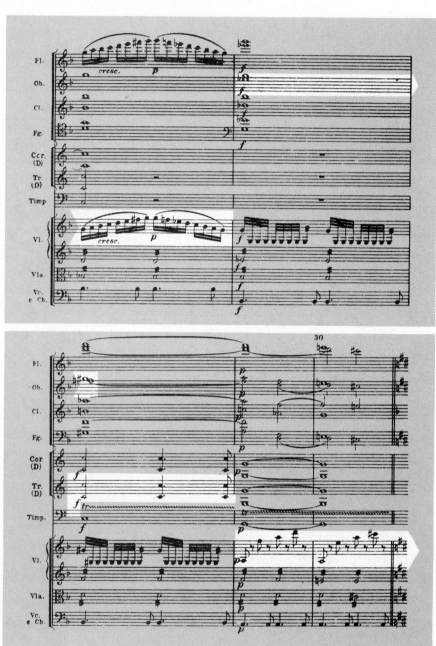

Molto allegro

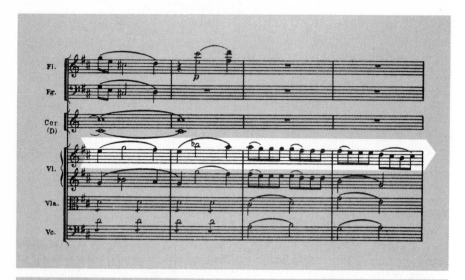

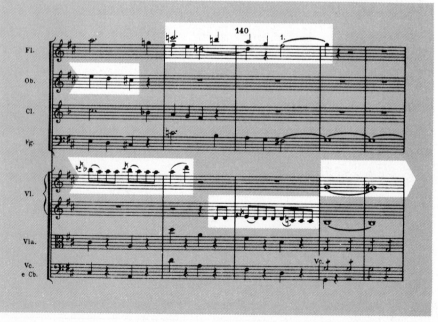

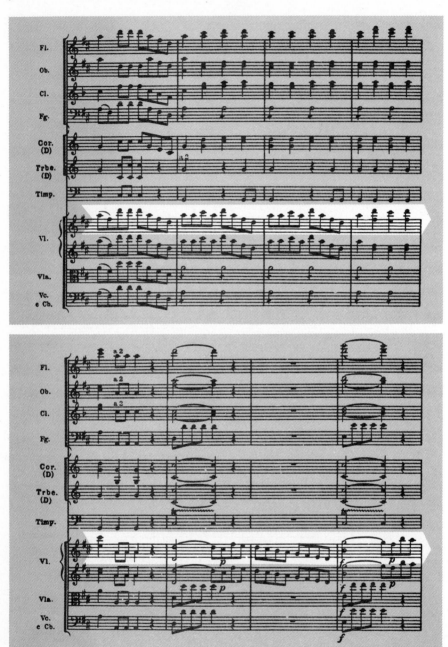

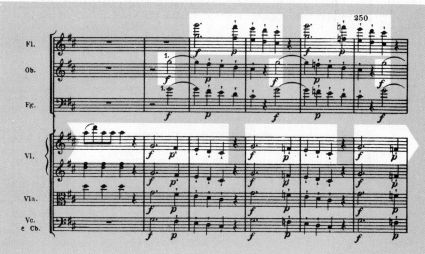

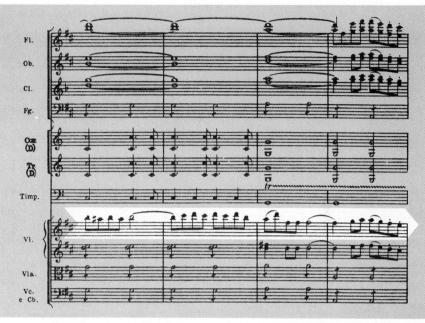

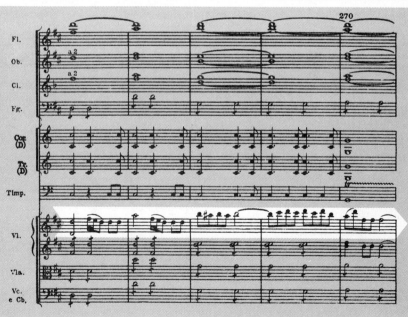

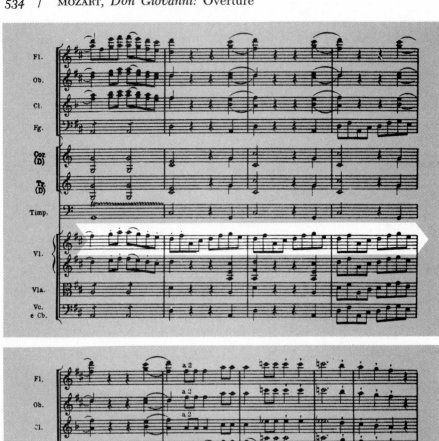

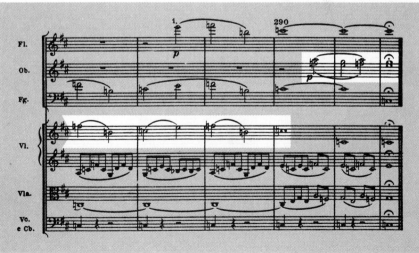

No. 1: Introduction

Scene— A Garden, Night.

Leporello, in a cloak, discovered watching before the house of Donna Anna; then Donna Anna and Don Giovanni, afterwards the Commandant.

(wrapt in a dark mantle, impatiently pacing to and fro before the steps to the palace).

Leporello.

Not-te e gior-no fa-ti - car, per chi nul-la sa gra - dir; pio-va e
On the go from morn till night, Run-ning er-rands, nev-er free, Hard-ly

ven - to sop-por - tar, mangiar ma-le, e mal dor - mir!
time to snatch a bite; This is not the life for me.

Vo - glio far il gen-til - uo - mo, e non
I would like to play the mas-ter, Would no

No. 4: *Catalogue Aria*

marchesa - ne, prin-ci-pesse, e v'han don-ne d'o-gni gra-do, d'o-gni for-ma, d'ogni e-
In the ranks of his suc-cess-es, Ev-'ry pos-si-ble con-di-tion, Oc-cu-pa-tion, form and

cresc.

tà, d'o-gni for-ma, d'o-gni e-tà, In I-ta-li-a
age All a-rouse his gal-lant rage! In A-ra-bi-a,

f *p* *vln.* *Cello & Bass*

sei cen-to e qua-ran-ta, in Al-ma-gna
ten doz-en were fool-ish; In Dal-ma-tia,

due cen-to e trent' u-na, cen - - to in Fran-cia, in Tur-
a hun-dred were wan-ton; Here's Hel-ve-tia— a

chia no-vant' u-na, ma, ma,— ma in I-spa-gna! ma in I-
gross in each Can-ton; But, but,— but o-ver-prud-ish Spain con-

No. 7: Duet: *Là ci darem la mano*

(Donna Elvira descends the steps, and posts herself at centre, back.)

in - no - cen - te a - mor!
in - no - cent - ly still.   (Exeunt, arm in arm.)

33. LUDWIG VAN BEETHOVEN (1770-1827),
First movement from *String Quartet in F major*,
Op. 18, No. 1 (1798-1799)

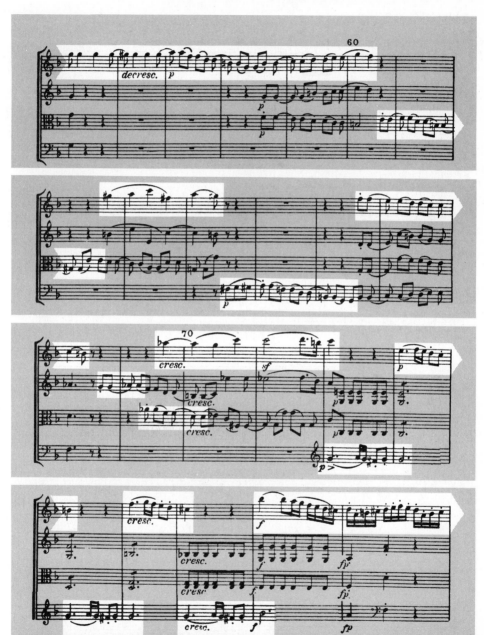

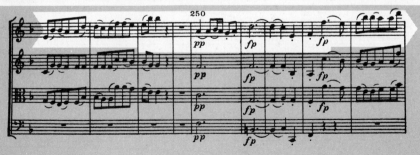

16-2

34. BEETHOVEN,
Piano Sonata in C minor, Op. 13 *(Pathétique)* (1799)

attacca subito il Allegro.

Tempo I.

attacca subito Allegro molto e con brio.

Allegro molto e con brio.

RONDO.
Allegro.

35. BEETHOVEN, *Symphony No. 5 in C minor* (1807)

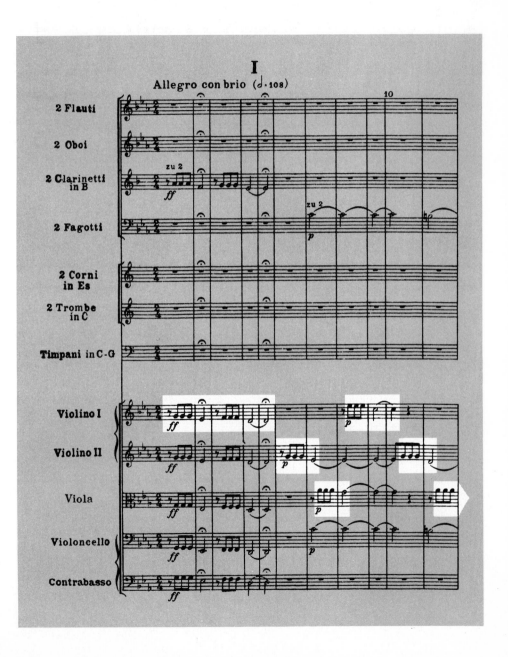

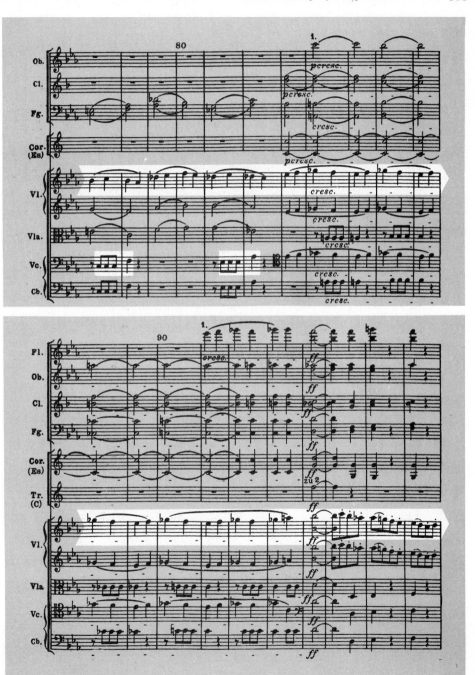

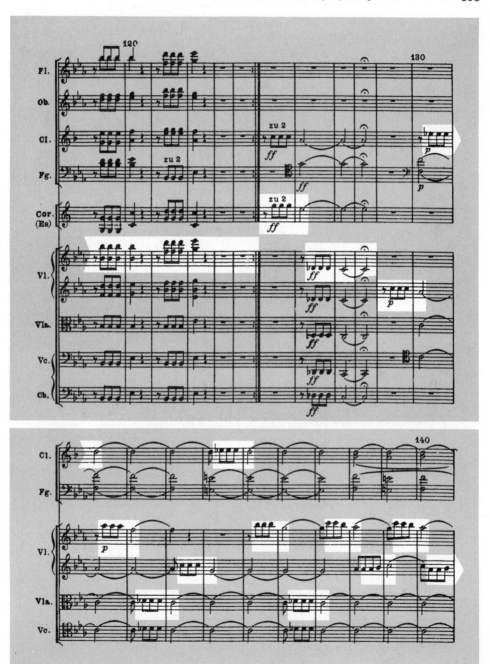

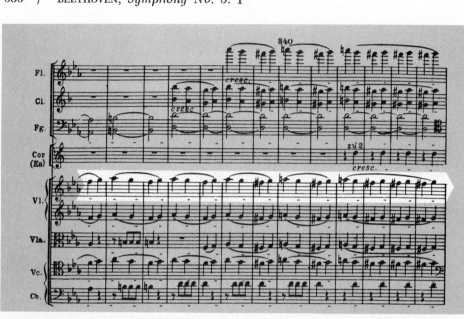

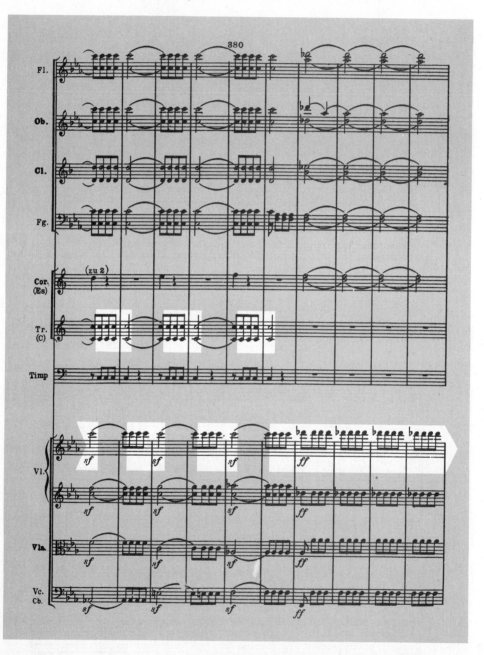

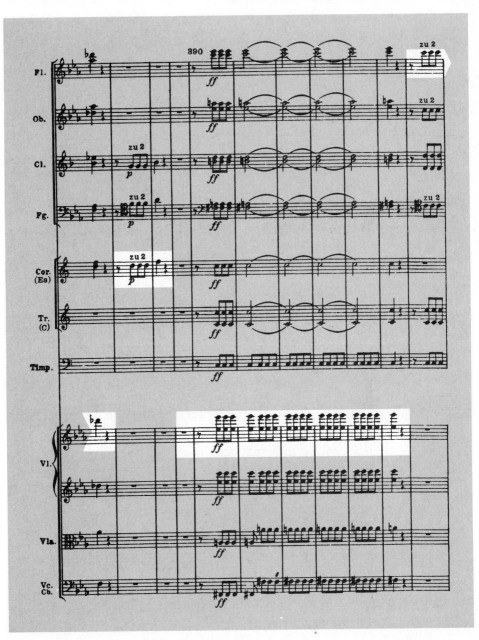

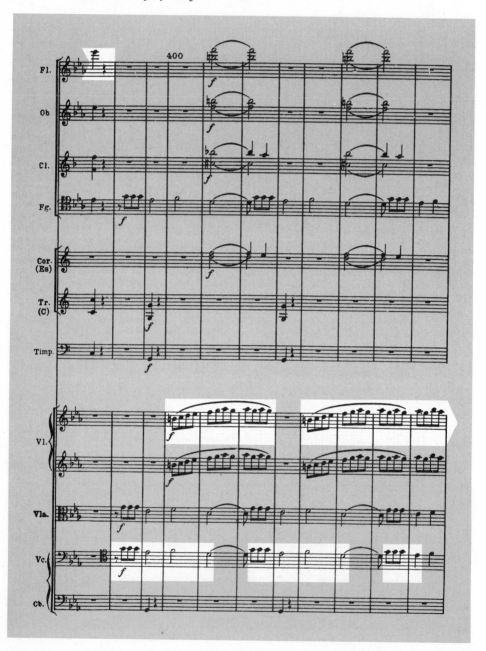

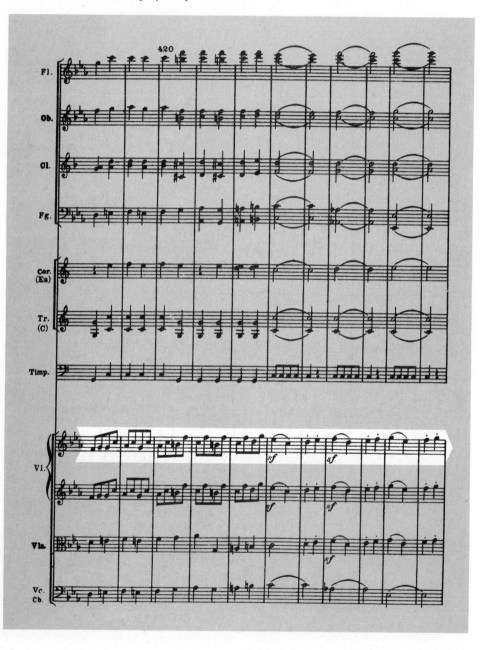

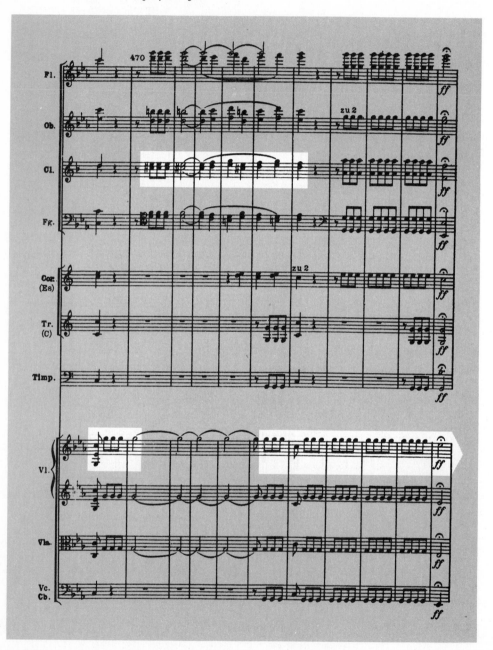

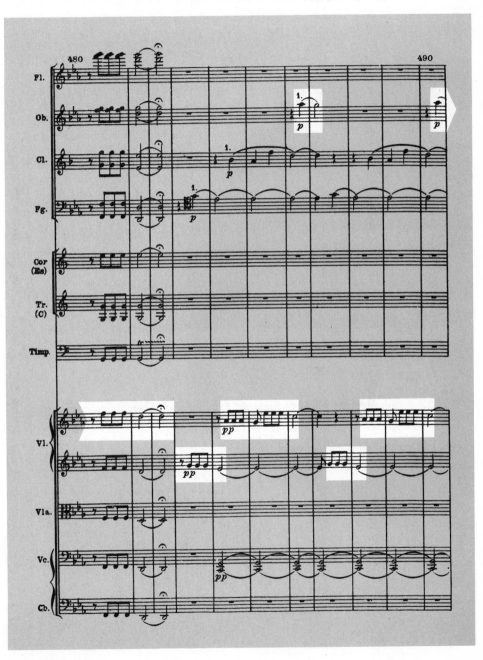

II

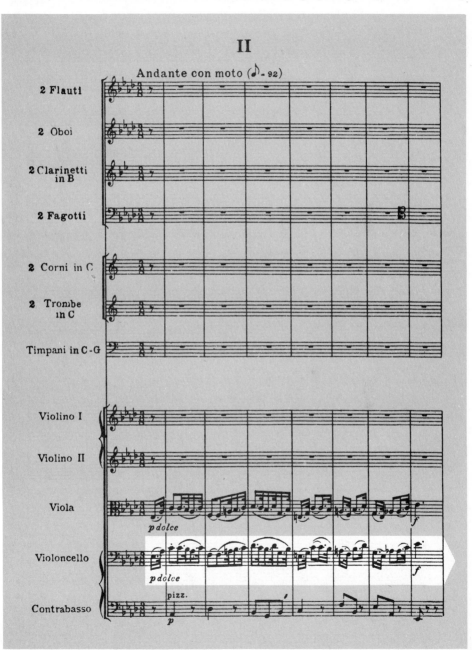

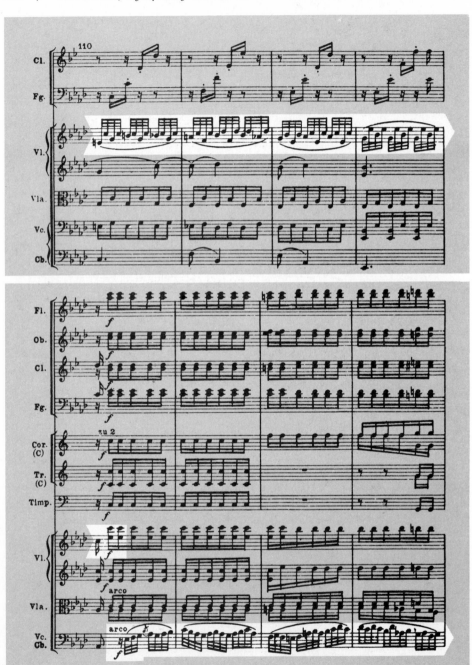

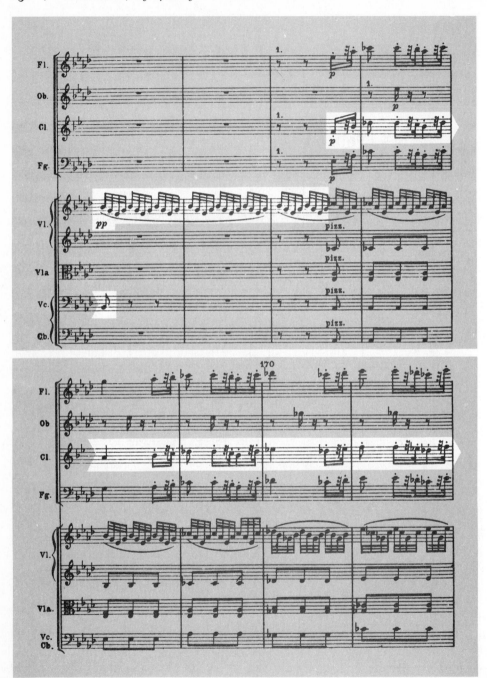

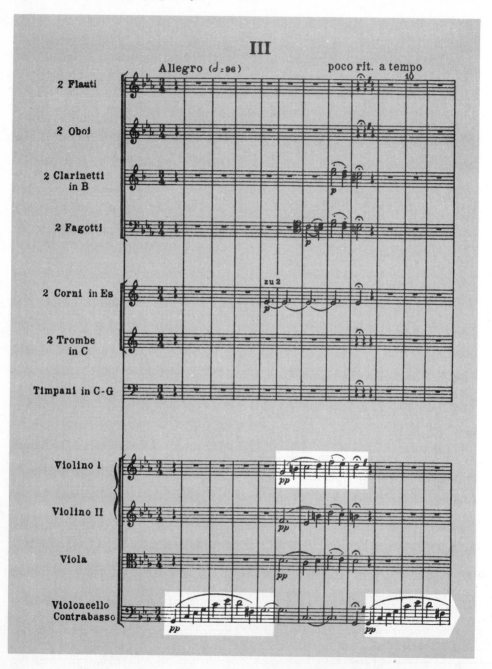

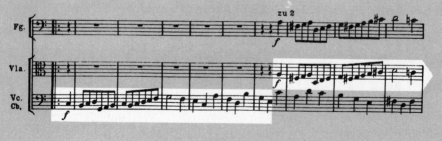

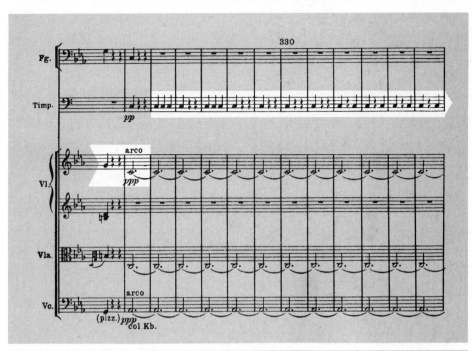

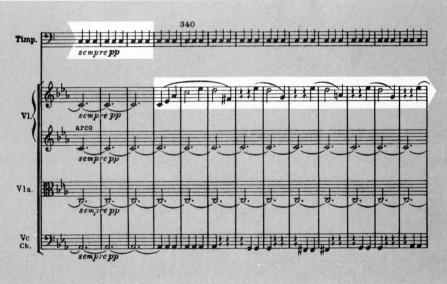

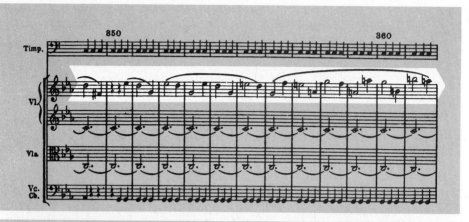

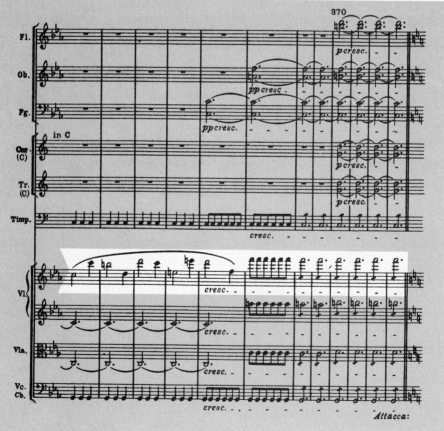

IV

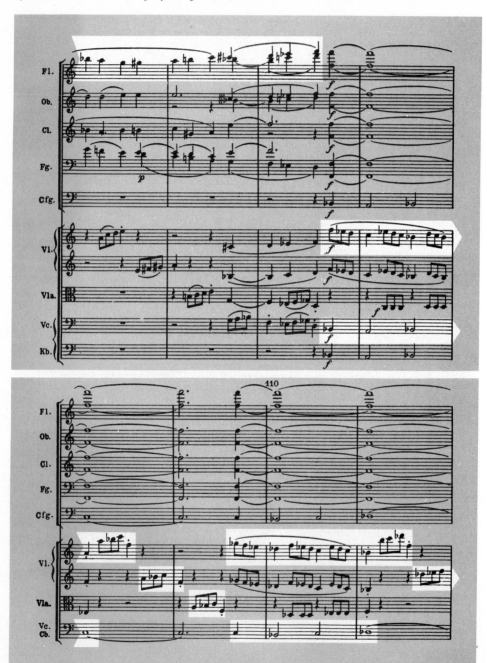

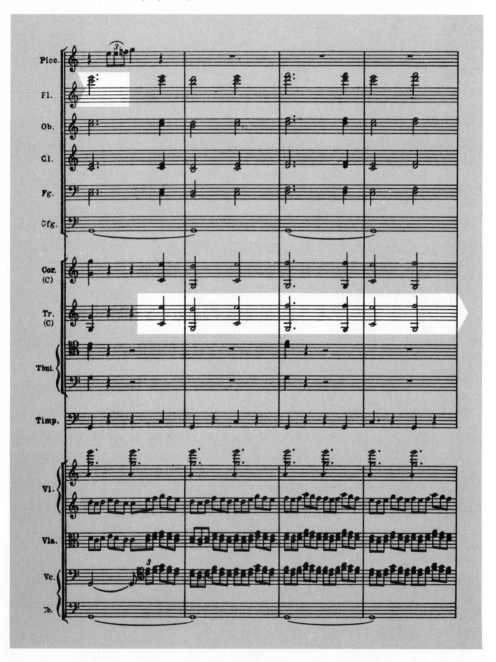

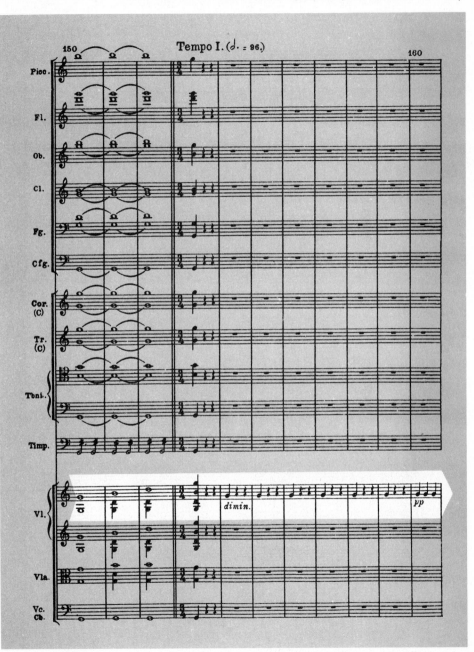

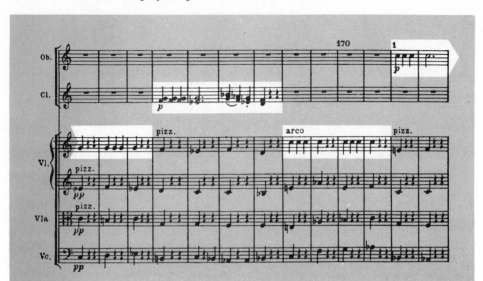

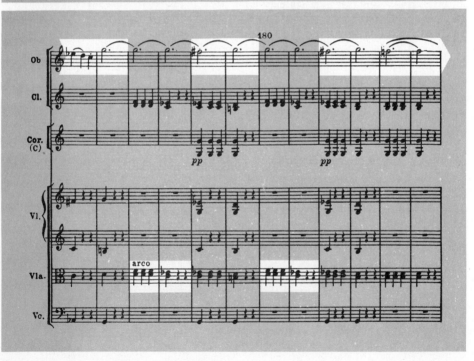

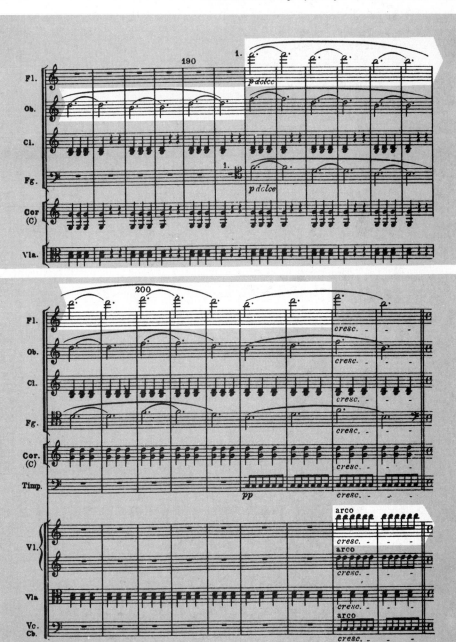

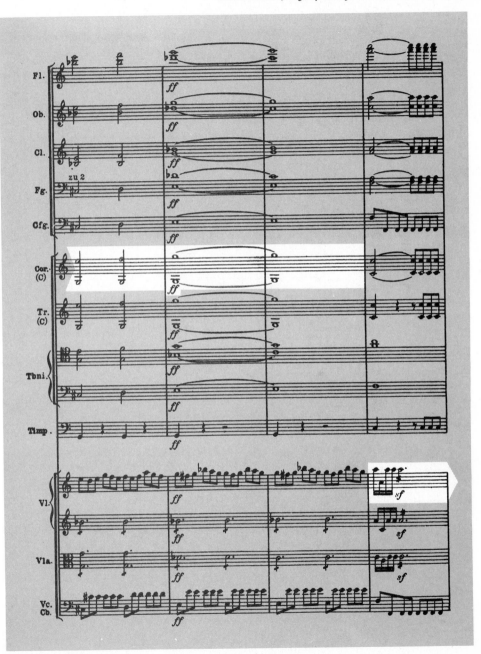

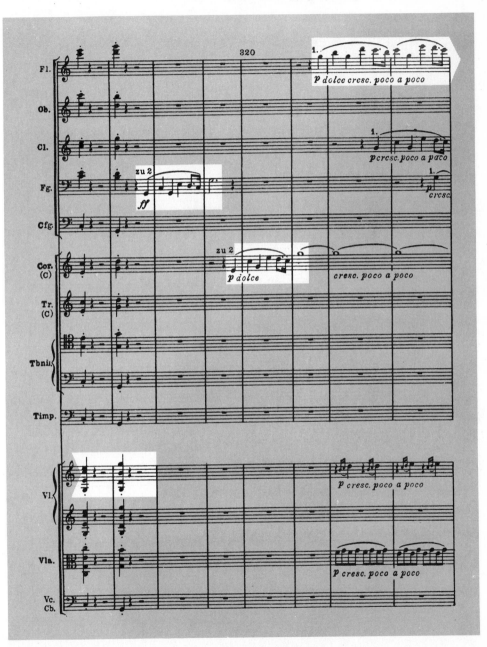

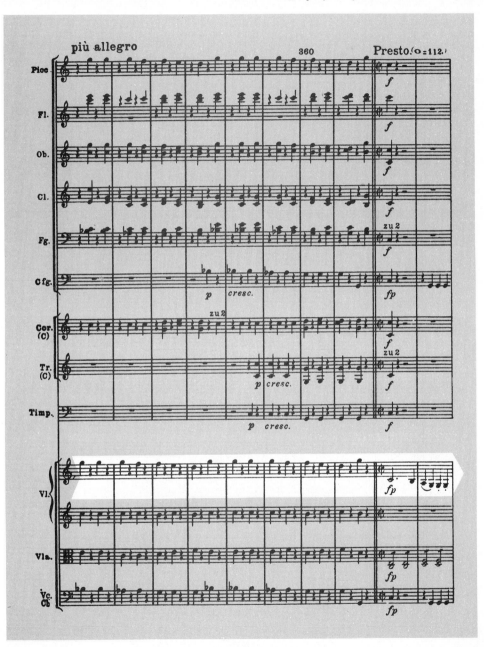

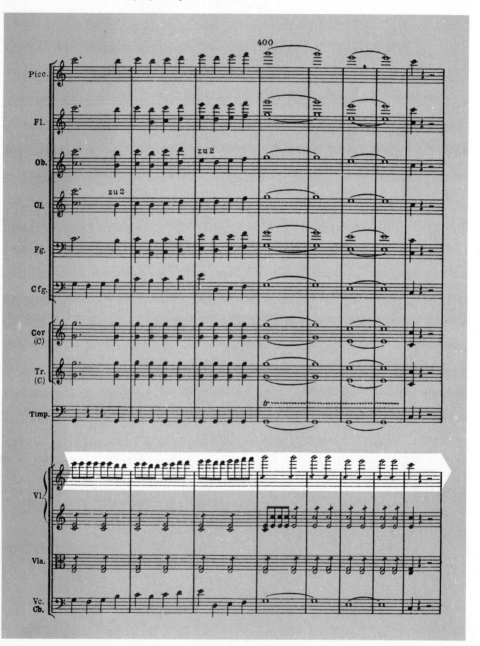

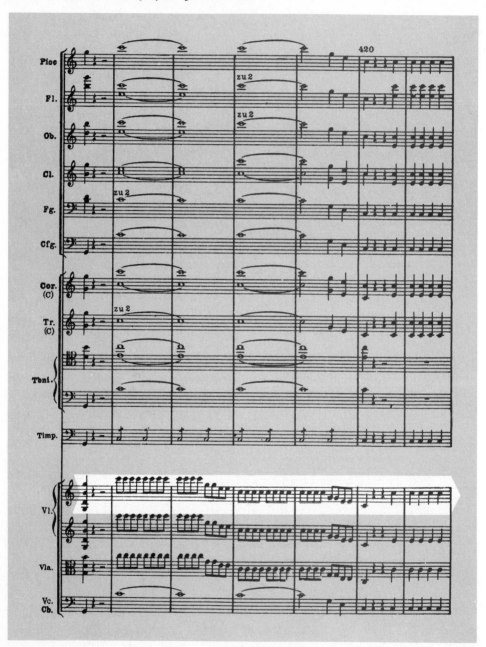

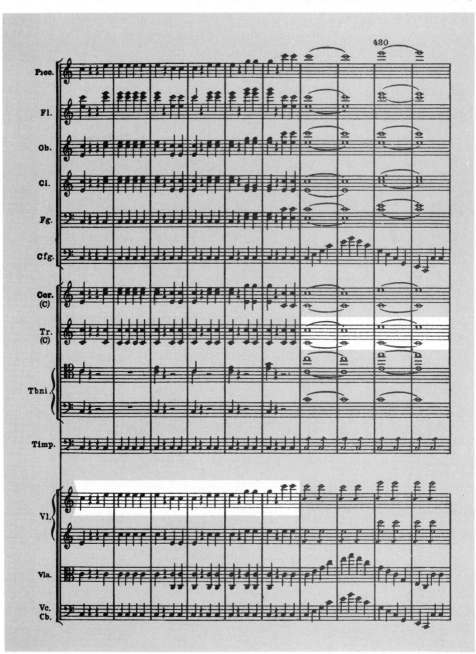

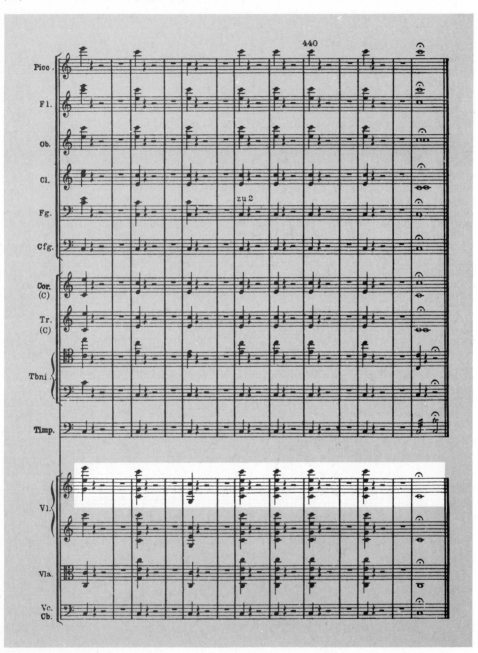

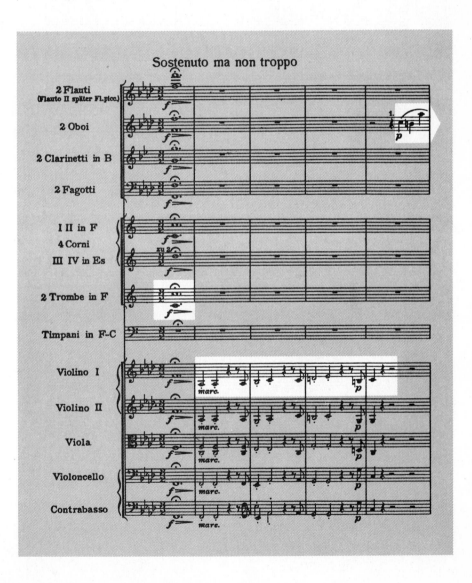

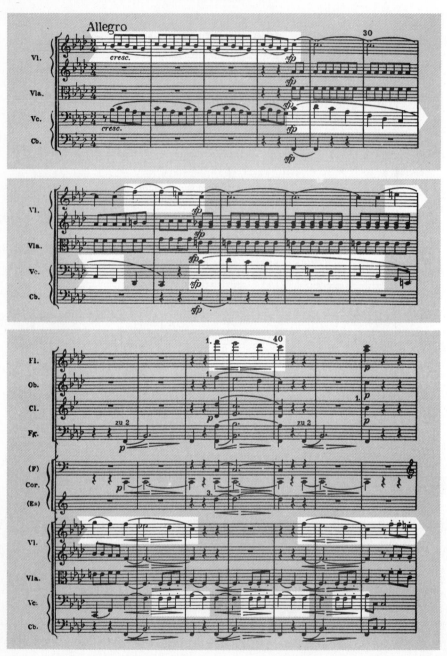

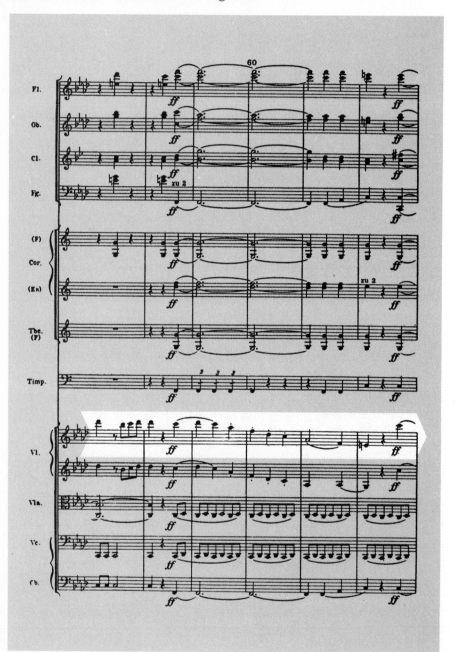

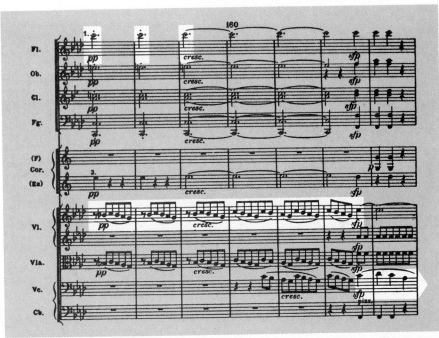

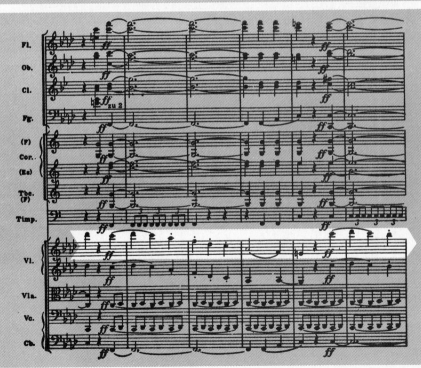

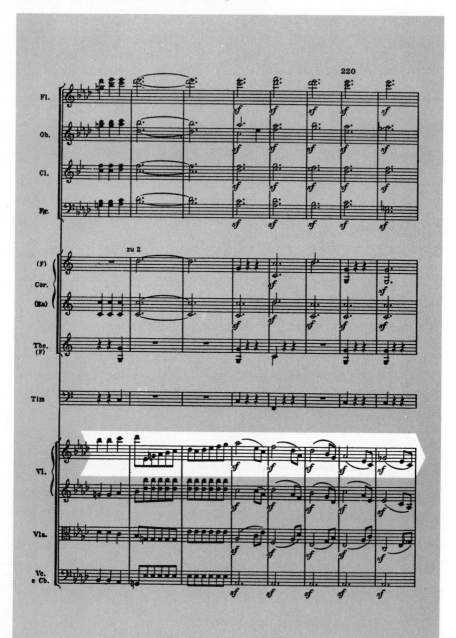

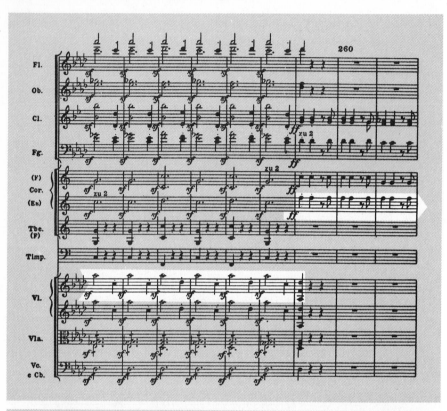

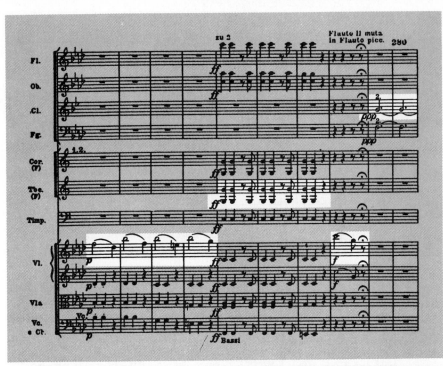

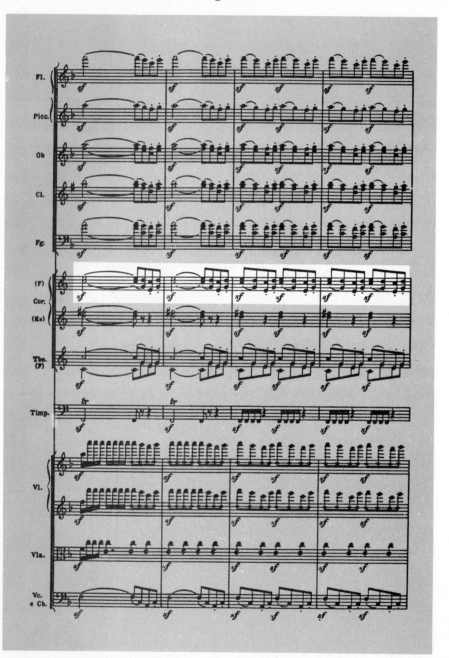

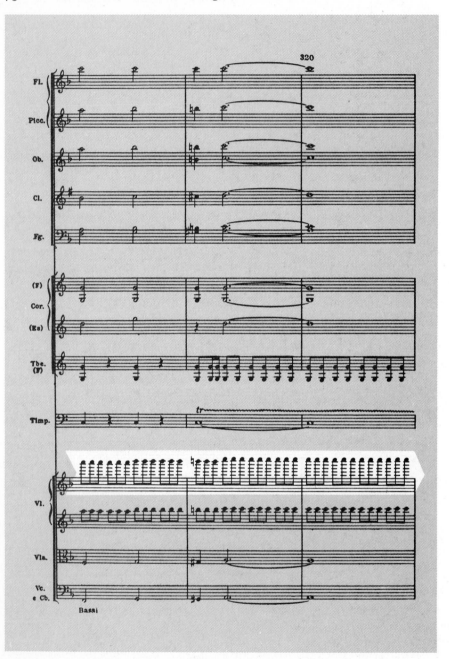

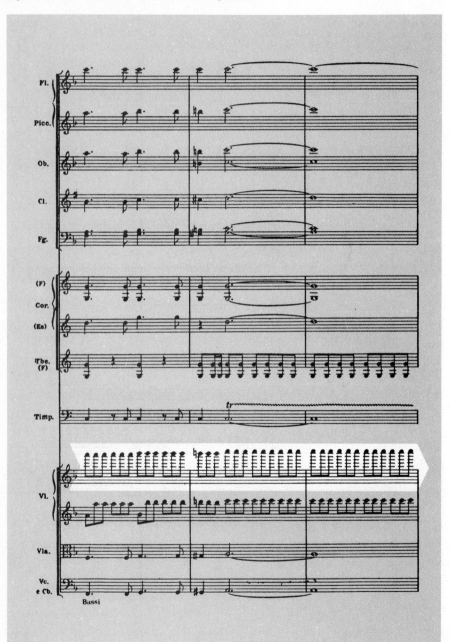

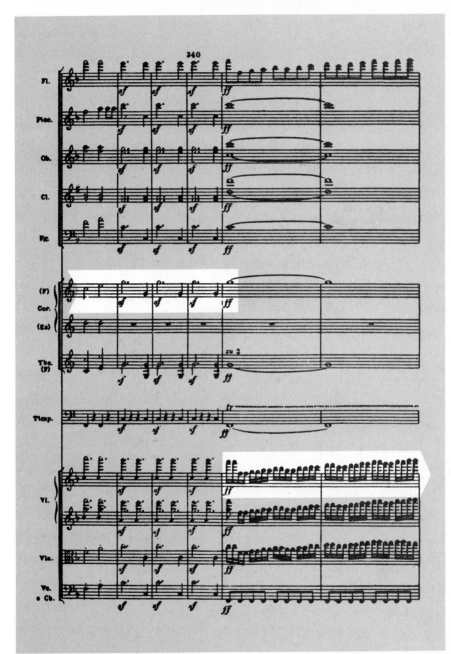

Appendix A

Reading an Orchestral Score

CLEFS

The music for some instruments is written in clefs other than the familiar treble and bass. In the following example, middle C is shown in the four clefs used in orchestral scores:

Treble
clef

Alto
clef

Tenor
clef

Bass
clef

The *alto clef* is primarily used in viola parts. The *tenor clef* is employed for cello, bassoon, and trombone parts when these instruments play in a high register.

TRANSPOSING INSTRUMENTS

The music for some instruments is customarily written at a pitch different from their actual sound. The following list, with examples, shows the main transposing instruments and the degree of transposition. (In some modern works—such as the Schoenberg example included in this anthology —all instruments are written at their sounding pitch.)

Instrument	Transposition	Written Note	Actual Sound
Piccolo Celesta	sound an octave higher than written		
Trumpet in F	sound a fourth higher than written		
Trumpet in E	sound a major third higher than written		

Instrument	*Transposition*	*Written Note*	*Actual Sound*

Clarinet in Eb
  Trumpet in Eb
	sound a minor third
	  higher than written		

Trumpet in D
  Clarinet in D
	sound a major second
	  higher than written		

Clarinet in Bb
  Trumpet in Bb
  Cornet in Bb
  Horn in Bb alto
	sound a major second
	  lower than written		

Clarinet in A
  Trumpet in A
  Cornet in A
	sound a minor third
	  lower than written		

Horn in G
  Alto flute
	sound a fourth
	  lower than written		

English horn
  Horn in F
	sound a fifth
	  lower than written		

Horn in E	sound a minor sixth lower than written		
Horn in Eb	sound a major sixth lower than written		
Horn in D	sound a minor seventh lower than written		

Contrabassoon
  Horn in C
  Double bass
	sound an octave
	  lower than written		

Bass clarinet in Bb
  (written in treble clef)
	sound a major ninth
	  lower than written		

(written in bass clef)	sound a major second lower than written		

Bass clarinet in A
  (written in treble clef)
	sound a minor tenth
	  lower than written		

(written in bass clef)	sound a minor third lower than written		

Appendix B

Instrumental Names and Abbreviations

The following tables set forth the English, Italian, German, and French names used for the various musical instruments in these scores, and their respective abbreviations. A table of the foreign-language names for scale degrees and modes is also provided.

WOODWINDS

English	Italian	German	French
Piccolo (Picc.)	Flauto piccolo (Fl. Picc.)	Kleine Flöte (Kl. Fl.)	Petite flûte
Flute (Fl.)	Flauto (Fl.); Flauto grande (Fl. gr.)	Grosse Flöte (Fl. gr.)	Flûte (Fl.)
Alto flute	Flauto contralto (fl.c-alto)	Altflöte	Flûte en sol
Oboe (Ob.)	Oboe (Ob.)	Hoboe (Hb.); Oboe (Ob.)	Hautbois (Hb.)
English horn (E. H.)	Corno inglese (C. or Cor. ingl., C.i.)	Englisches Horn (E. H.)	Cor anglais (C. A.)
Sopranino clarinet	Clarinetto piccolo (clar. picc.)		
Clarinet (C., Cl., Clt., Clar.)	Clarinetto (Cl. Clar.)	Klarinette (Kl.)	Clarinette (Cl.)
Bass clarinet (B. Cl.)	Clarinetto basso (Cl. b., Cl. basso, Clar. basso)	Bass Klarinette (Bkl.)	Clarinette basse (Cl. bs.)
Bassoon (Bsn., Bssn.)	Fagotto (Fag., Fg.)	Fagott (Fag., Fg.)	Basson (Bssn.)
Contrabassoon (C. Bsn.)	Contrafagotto (Cfg., C. Fag., Cont. F.)	Kontrafagott (Kfg.)	Contrebasson (C. bssn.)

BRASS

English	*Italian*	*German*	*French*
French horn (Hr., Hn.)	Corno (Cor., C.)	Horn (Hr.) [*pl.* Hörner (Hrn.)]	Cor; Cor à pistons
Trumpet (Tpt., Trpt., Trp., Tr.)	Tromba (Tr.)	Trompete (Tr., Trp.)	Trompette (Tr.)
Trumpet in D	Tromba piccola (Tr. picc.)		
Cornet	Cornetta	Kornett	Cornet à pistons (C. à p., Pist.)
Trombone (Tr., Tbe., Trb., Trm., Trbe.)	Trombone [*pl.* Tromboni (Tbni., Trni.)]	Posaune (Ps., Pos.)	Trombone (Tr.)
Tuba (Tb.)	Tuba (Tb, Tba:)	Tuba (Tb.) [*also* Basstuba (Btb.)]	Tuba (Tb.)

PERCUSSION

English	*Italian*	*German*	*French*
Percussion (Perc.)	Percussione	Schlagzeug (Schlag.)	Batterie (Batt.)
Kettledrums (K. D.)	Timpani (Timp., Tp.)	Pauken (Pk.)	Timbales (Timb.)
Snare drum (S. D.)	Tamburo piccolo (Tamb. picc.) Tamburo militare (Tamb. milit.)	Kleine Trommel (Kl. Tr.)	Caisse claire (C. cl.), Caisse roulante Tambour militaire (Tamb. milit.)
Bass drum (B. drum)	Gran cassa (Gr. Cassa, Gr. C., G. C.)	Grosse Trommel (Gr. Tr.)	Grosse caisse (Gr. c.)
Cymbals (Cym., Cymb.)	Piatti (P., Ptti., Piat.)	Becken (Beck.)	Cymbales (Cym.)
Tam-Tam (Tam-T.)			
Tambourine (Tamb.)	Tamburino (Tamb.)	Schellentrommel, Tamburin	Tambour de Basque (T. de B., Tamb. de Basque)

Triangle (Trgl., Tri.)	Triangolo (Trgl.)	Triangel	Triangle (Triang.)
Glockenspiel (Glocken.)	Campanelli (Cmp.)	Glockenspiel	Carillon
Bells (Chimes)	Campane (Cmp.)	Glocken	Cloches
Antique Cymbals	Crotali Piatti antichi	Antiken Zimbeln	Cymbales antiques
Sleigh Bells	Sonagli (Son.)	Schellen	Grelots
Xylophone (Xyl.)	Xilofono	Xylophon	Xylophone
Cowbells		Herdenglocken	
Crash cymbal			Grande cymbale chinoise
Siren			Sirène
Lion's roar			Tambour à corde
Slapstick			Fouet
Wood blocks			Blocs chinois

STRINGS

English	*Italian*	*German*	*French*
Violin (V., Vl., Vln, Vi.)	Violino (V., Vl., Vln.)	Violine (V., Vl., Vln.) Geige (Gg.)	Violon (V., Vl., Vln.)
Viola (Va., Vl., pl. Vas.)	Viola (Va., Vla.) pl. Viole (Vle.)	Bratsche (Br.)	Alto (A.)
Violoncello, Cello (Vcl., Vc.)	Violoncello (Vc., Vlc., Vcllo.)	Violoncell (Vc., Vlc.)	Violoncelle (Vc.)
Double bass (D. Bs.)	Contrabasso (Cb., C. B.) pl. Contrabassi or Bassi (C. Bassi, Bi.)	Kontrabass (Kb.)	Contrebasse (C. B.)

OTHER INSTRUMENTS

English	*Italian*	*German*	*French*
Harp (Hp., Hrp.)	Arpa (A., Arp.)	Harfe (Hrf.)	Harpe (Hp.)
Piano	Pianoforte (P.-f., Pft.)	Klavier	Piano
Celesta (Cel.)			
Harpsichord	Cembalo	Cembalo	Clavecin
Harmonium (Harmon.)			
Organ (Org.)	Organo	Orgel	Orgue
Guitar		Gitarre (Git.)	
Mandoline (Mand.)			

Names of Scale Degrees and Modes

SCALE DEGREES

English	Italian	German	French
C	do	C	ut
C-sharp	do diesis	Cis	ut dièse
D-flat	re bemolle	Des	ré bémol
D	re	D	ré
D-sharp	re diesis	Dis	ré dièse
E-flat	mi bemolle	Es	mi bémol
E	mi	E	mi
E-sharp	mi diesis	Eis	mi dièse
F-flat	fa bemolle	Fes	fa bémol
F	fa	F	fa
F-sharp	fa diesis	Fis	fa dièse
G-flat	sol bemolle	Ges	sol bémol
G	sol	G	sol
G-sharp	sol diesis	Gis	sol dièse
A-flat	la bemolle	As	la bémol
A	la	A	la
A-sharp	la diesis	Ais	la dièse
B-flat	si bemolle	B	si bémol
B	si	H	si
B-sharp	si diesis	His	si dièse
C-flat	do bemolle	Ces	ut bémol

MODES

major	maggiore	dur	majeur
minor	minore	moll	mineur

Note on Baroque Instruments

In the Baroque works, certain older instruments, not used in the modern orchestra, were required by the composers; the following list defines these terms.

Continuo (Con.) A method of indicating an accompanying part by the bass notes only, together with figures designating the chords to be played above them. In general practice, the chords are played on a harpsichord or organ, while a viola da gamba or cello doubles the bass notes.

and a bass lute (as continuo instruments).

Corno. Although this term usually designates the French horn, in the Bach Cantata No. 140 it refers to the *cornett*, or *zink*—a wooden trumpet without valves.

Taille (Tail.). In the Bach Cantata No. 140, this term indicates a tenor oboe or English horn.

Violino piccolo. A small violin, tuned a fourth higher than the standard violin.

Violone (V.). A string instrument intermediate in size between the cello and the double bass. (In modern performances, the double bass is commonly substituted.)

Appendix C

Glossary of Musical Terms Used in the Scores

The following glossary is not intended to be a complete dictionary of musical terms, nor is knowledge of all these terms necessary to follow the scores in this book. However, as the listener gains experience in following scores, he will find it useful and interesting to understand the composer's directions with regard to tempo, dynamics, and methods of performance.

In most cases, compound terms have been broken down in the glossary and defined separately, as they often recur in varying combinations. A few common foreign-language particles are included in addition to the musical terms. Note that names and abbreviations for instruments and for scale degrees will be found in Appendix B.

a. The phrases *a 2, a 3* (etc.) indicate that the part is to be played in unison by 2, 3 (etc.) players; when a simple number (1., 2., etc.) is placed over a part, it indicates that only the first (second, etc.) player in that group should play.

aber. But.

accelerando. Growing faster.

accentué. Accented.

accompagnato (accomp.). In a continuo part, this indicates that the chord-playing instrument resumes (cf. *tasto solo*).

accordez. Tune the instrument as specified.

adagio. Slow, leisurely.

ad libitum (ad lib.). An indication giving the performer liberty to: (1) vary from strict tempo; (2) include or omit the part of some voice or instrument; (3) include a cadenza of his own invention.

affettuoso. With emotion.

affrettando (affrett.). Hastening a little.

agitato. Agitated, excited.

agitazione. Agitation.

allargando (allarg.). Growing broader.

alle, alles. All, every, each.

allegretto. A moderately fast tempo (between allegro and andante).

allegro. A rapid tempo (between allegretto and presto).

allein. Alone, solo.

allmählich. Gradually (*allmählich gleichmässig fliessend werden,* gradually becoming even-flowing again).

al niente. Reduce to nothing.

alto, altus (A.). The deeper of the two main divisions of women's (or boys') voices.

alzate. Indication to remove mutes.

am Steg. On the bridge (of a string instrument).

ancora. Again.

andante. A moderately slow tempo (between adagio and allegretto).

andantino. A moderately slow tempo.

an dem Griffbrett (a.d.G.). Played on the fingerboard.

Anfang. Beginning.

anima. Spirit, animation.

animando. With increasing animation.

animato, animé. Animated.

anschwellend. Crescendo.

a piacere. The execution of the passage is left to the performer's discretion.

à plat. Laid flat.

appassionato. Impassioned.

arco. Played with the bow.

arditamente. Boldly.

armonioso. Harmoniously.

arpeggiando, arpeggiato (arpeg.). Played in harp style, i.e. the notes of the chord played in quick succession rather than simultaneously.

arrêt. Stop.

assai. Very.

a tempo. At the (basic) tempo.

attacca. Begin what follows without pausing.

attaque sèche. Sharp attack.

auf dem. On the (as in *auf dem G,* on the G string).

Ausdruck. Expression.

ausdrucksvoll. With expression.

äusserst. Extreme, utmost.

bachetti. Drumsticks (*bachetti di tamburo militare,* snare-drum sticks; *bachetti di spugna,* sponge-headed drumsticks).

baguettes. Drumsticks (*baguettes de bois, baguettes timbales de bois,* wooden drumsticks or kettledrum sticks; *baguettes d'éponge,* sponge-headed drumsticks; *baguettes mi-dures,* semi-hard drumsticks; *baguettes dures,* hard drumsticks; *baguettes timbales en feutre,* felt-headed kettledrum sticks).

bass, basso, bassus (B.). The lowest male voice.

battuto coll' arco. Struck with the bow.

beaucoup. Many, much.

Becken. Cymbals.

bedeutung bewegter. With significantly more movement.

beide Hände. With both hands.

belebend. With increasing animation.

belebt. Animated.

ben. Very.

ben accordato. Well tuned.

bestimmt. Energetic.

bewegt. Agitated.

bewegter. More agitated.

bien. Very.

bis zum Schluss dieser Szene. To the end of this scene.

Blech. Brass instruments.

Bogen (Bog.). Played with the bow.

bouché. Muted.

bravura. Boldness.

breit. Broadly.

breiter. More broadly.

brillante. Brilliant.

brio. Spirit, vivacity.

cadenza. An extended passage for solo instrument in free, improvisatory style.

calando. Diminishing in volume and speed.

calma, calmo. Calm, calmly.

cantabile (cant.). In a singing style.

cantando. In a singing manner.

canto. Voice (as in *col canto,* a direction for the accompaniment to follow the solo part in tempo and expression).

cantus. An older designation for the highest part in a vocal work.

capella. Choir, chorus.

cédez. Go a little slower.

changez. Change (usually an instruction to re-tune a string or an instrument).

circa (ca.). About, approximately.

clair. High.

col, colla, coll'. With the.

come prima, come sopra. As at first; as previously.

comodo. Comfortable, easy.

con. With.

corda. String; for example, *seconda (2a) corda* is the second string (the A string on the violin).

coro. Chorus.

coulisse. Wings (of a theater).

court. Short, staccato.

crescendo (cresc.). An increase in volume.

cuivré. Played with a harsh, blaring tone.

cum quatuor vocibus. With four voices.

cupo. Dark, veiled.

dabei. Thereby, therewith; at the same time.

da capo (D.C.). Repeat from the beginning.

dal segno. Repeat from the sign.

Dämpfer (Dpf.). Mutes.

dans. In.

dazu. In addition to that, for that purpose.

début. Beginning.

decrescendo (decresc., decr.). A decreasing of volume.

descendez le "la" un demi-ton plus bas. Lower the A-string a semitone.

détaché. With a broad, vigorous bow stroke, each note bowed singly.

détimbrée. With snares (of a snare drum) relaxed.

deutlich. Distinctly.

devozione. Devotion; affection, reverence.

dimenuendo, diminuer (dim., dimin.). A decreasing of volume.

distinto. Distinct, clear.

divisés, divisi (div.). Divided; indicates that the instrumental group should be divided into two parts to play the passage in question.

dolce. Sweetly and softly.

dolcemente. Sweetly.

dolcezza. Sweetness; gentleness.

dolcissimo (dolciss.). Very sweetly.

dolente. Sorrowful.

dopo. After, afterwards.

Doppelgriff. Double stop.

doppio movimento. Twice as fast.

doux. Sweetly.

drängend. Pressing on.

duplum. In older music, the part immediately above the tenor.

durée indiquée. The duration indicated.

e. And.

eilen. To hurry.

elegante. Elegant, graceful.

en animant. Becoming more animated.

enchainez. Continue to the next material without pause.

en dehors. With emphasis.

energico. Energetically.

entsprechend. Appropriate; corresponding.

ersterbend. Dying away.

erstes Tempo. At the original tempo.

espansione. Expansion, broadening.

espressione. With expression.

espressione intensa. Intense expression.

espressivo (espress., espr.). Expressively.

et. And.

etwas. Somewhat, rather.

expressif. Expressively.

fehlende Akkordtöne. Missing chord tones.

feroce. Fierce, ferocious.

fiero. Fiercely.

fine. End, close.

Flageolett (Flag.). Harmonics.

flatterzunge, flutter-tongue. A special tonguing technique for wind instruments, producing a rapid trill-like sound.

flebile. Feeble; plaintive; mournful.

fliessend. Flowing.

forte (f). Loud.

fortissimo (ff). Very loud (*fff* indicates a still louder dynamic).

forza. Force.

frei. Freely.

freihäng. Hanging freely. An indication to the percussionist to let the cymbals vibrate feely.

frottez. Rub.

früher. Earlier; former.

fuga. Fugue.

fuoco. Fire, spirit.

furioso. Furiously.

Fuss. Foot; pedal.

gajo. Gaily.

ganz. Entirely, altogether.

ganzton. Whole tone.

gedämpft (ged.). Muted.

geheimnisvoll. Mysteriously.

gesteigert. Intensified.

gestopft (chiuso). Stopping the notes of a horn; that is, the hand is placed in the bell of the horn, to produce a muffled sound.

geteilt (get.). Divided; indicates that the instrumental group should be divided into two parts to play the passage in question.

giocoso. Jocose, humorous.

giusto. Moderately.

gli altri. The others.

glissando (gliss.). Rapid scales produced by running the fingers over all the strings.

gradamente. Gradually.

grande. Large, great.

grande taille. Large size.

grandioso. Grandiose.

grave. Slow, solemn; deep, low.

grazia. Grace, charm.

grazioso. Gracefully.

grosser Auftakt. Big upbeat.

gut gehalten. Well sustained.

H. A symbol used in the music of Schoenberg, Berg, and Webern to indicate the most important voice in the texture.

Hälfte. Half.

harmonic (harm.). A flute-like sound produced on a string instrument by lightly touching the string with the finger instead of pressing it down.

Hauptzeitmass. Original tempo.

heimlich. Furtively.

hervortretend. Prominent.

hoch. High; nobly.

Holz. Woodwinds.

im gleichen Rhythmus. In the same rhythm.

immer chromatisch. Always chromatic.

immer im Tempo. Always in tempo.

incalzando. Pressing, hurrying.

in neuen Tempo. In the new tempo.

istesso tempo. Duration of beat remains unaltered despite meter change.

jeté. With a bouncing motion of the bow.

jusqu'à la fin. To the end.

kadenzieren. To cadence.

kaum hörbar. Barely audible.

klagend. Lamenting.

Klang. Sound; timbre.

kleine. Little.

kurz. Short.

laissez vibrer. Let vibrate; an indication to the player of a harp, cymbal, etc., that the sound must not be damped.

lamentoso. Plaintive, mournful.

langsam. Slow.

langsamer. Slower.

languente. Languishing.

langueur. Languor.

largamente. Broadly.

larghetto. Slightly faster than largo.

largo. A very slow tempo.

lebhaft. Lively.

leere Bühne. Empty stage.

legatissimo. A more forceful indication of *legato.*

legato. Performed without any perceptible interruption between notes.

légèrement. Lightly.

leggèro, leggiero (legg.). Light and graceful.

legno. The wood of the bow *(col legno tratto,* bowed with the wood; *col legno battuto,* tapped with the wood; *col legno gestrich,* played with the wood).

leise. Soft, low.

lent. Slowly.

lentamente. Slowly.

lento. A slow tempo (between andante and largo).

l.h. Abbreviation for "left hand."

licenza. With license.

lieblich. Lovely, sweetly.

l'istesso tempo, see *istesso tempo.*

loco. Indicates a return to the written pitch, following a passage played an octave higher or lower than written.

lontano. Far away, from a distance.

luftpause. Pause for breath.

lunga. Long, sustained.

lungo silenzio. A long pause.

lusingando. Caressing.

ma. But.

maestoso. Majestic.

manual. A keyboard played with the hands (as ·distinct from the pedal keyboard on an organ).

marcatissimo (marcatiss.). With very marked emphasis.

marcato (marc.). Marked, with emphasis.

marcia. March.

marqué. Marked, with emphasis.

marziale. Military, martial, march-like.

mässig. Moderate.

Melodie. Melody, tune, air.

même. Same.

meno. Less.

mezza voce. With half the voice power.

mezzo forte (mf). Moderately loud.

mezzo piano (mp). Moderately soft.

mindistens. At least.

minore. In the minor mode.

misterioso. Misterious.

mit. With.

M. M. Metronome; followed by an indication of the setting for the correct tempo.

moderato, modéré. At a moderate tempo.

modo ordinario (ordin.). In the usual way (usually cancelling an instruction to play using some special technique).

möglich. Possible.

molto. Very, much.

morendo. Dying away.

mormorato. Murmured.

mosso. Rapid.

motetus. In medieval polyphonic music, a voice part above the tenor; generally, the first additional part to be composed.

moto. Motion.

mouvement (mouvt.). Tempo.

moyenne. Medium.

muta, mutano. Change the tuning of the instrument as specified.

N. A symbol used in the music of Schoenberg, Berg, and Webern to indicate the second most important voice in the texture.

nachgebend. Becoming slower.

Nachschlag. Grace-note that follows rather than precedes the note ornamented.

nach und nach. More and more.

naturalezza. A natural, unaffected manner.

naturel. In the usual way (generally cancelling an instruction to play using some special technique).

Nebenstimme. Subordinate or accompanying part.

nicht, non. Not.

noch. Still.

non. Not.

nuances. Shadings, expression.

oberer. Upper, leading.

octava (8va). Octave; if not otherwise qualified, means the notes marked should be played an octave higher than written.

octava bassa (8va bassa). Play an octave lower than written.

ohne. Without.

ondegg'ante. Undulating movement of the bow, which produces a tremolo effect.

open. (1) In brass instruments, the opposite of muted; (2) in string instruments, refers to the unstopped string (i.e. sounding at its full length).

ordinario, ordinérement (ordin.). In the usual way (generally cancelling an instruction to play using some special technique).

ossia. An alternative (usually easier) version of a passage.

ôtez vite les sourdines. Remove the mutes quickly.

ouvert. Open.

parlante. Sung in a manner resembling speech.

parte. Part (*colla parte*, the accompaniment is to follow the soloist in tempo).

pas trop long. Not too long.

Paukenschlägel. Timpani stick.

pavillon en l'aire. An indication to the player of a wind instrument to raise the bell of the instrument upward.

pedal (ped., P.). (1) In piano music, indicates that the damper pedal should be depressed; an asterisk indicates the point of release (brackets below the music are also used to indicate pedalling); (2) on an organ, the pedals are a keyboard played with the feet.

percutée. Percussive.

perdendosi. Gradually dying away.

pesante. Heavily.

peu. Little, a little.

pianissimo (pp). Very soft (*ppp* indicates a still softer dynamic).

piano (p). Soft.

piatto. Cymbal; flat, even; plain, dull.

più. More.

pizzicato (pizz.). The string plucked with the finger.

plötzlich. Suddenly, immediately.

plus. More.

pochissimo (pochiss.). Very little, a very little.

poco. Little, a little.

poco a poco. Little by little.

pomposo. Pompous.

ponticello (pont.). The bridge (of a string instrument).

portando la voce. With a smooth sliding of the voice from one tone to the next.

position naturel (pos. nat.). In the normal position (usually cancelling an instruction to play using some special technique).

possibile. Possible.

pouce. Thumb.

pour. For.

praeludium. Prelude.

premier mouvement (1er mouvt.). At the original tempo.

prenez. Take up.

préparez le ton. Prepare the instrument to play in the key named.

presser. To press.

presto. A very quick tempo (faster than allegro).

prima. First, principal.

principale (pr.). Principal, solo.

punta d'arco. Played with the top of the bow.

quasi. Almost, as if.

quasi niente. Almost nothing, i.e. as softly as possible.

quasi trill (tr.). In the manner of a trill.

quintus. An older designation for the fifth part in a vocal work.

rallentando (rall., rallent.). Growing slower.

rapide, rapido. Quick.

rapidissimo. Very quick.

rasch. Quick.

rauschend. Rustling, roaring.

recitative (recit.). A vocal style designed to imitate and emphasize the natural inflections of speech.

retenu. Held back.

revenir au Tempo. Return to the original tempo.

richtig. Correct (*richtige Lage,* correct pitch).

rigore di tempo. Strictness of tempo.

rigueur. Precision.

rinforzando (rf, rfz, rinf.). A sudden accent on a single note or chord.

risoluto. Determined.

ritardando (rit., ritard.). Gradually slackening in speed.

ritenuto (riten.). Immediate reduction of speed.

ronde. Round dance; whole note (Fr.).

rubato. A certain elasticity and flexibility of tempo, consisting of slight accelerandos and ritardandos according to the requirements of the musical expression.

ruhig. Quietly.

rullante. Rolling.

saltando (salt.). An indication to the string player to bounce the bow off the string by playing with short, quick bow-strokes.

sans timbre. Without snares.

scena vuota. Empty stage.

scherzando (scherz.). Playful.

schleppend. Dragging.

Schluss. Cadence, conclusion.

schmachtend. Languishing.

schnell. Fast.

schneller. Faster.

schon. Already.

schwächer. Weaker; milder; fainter.

schwer. Heavy, ponderous; grave, serious.

scorrevole. Flowing, gliding.

sec, secco. Dry, simple.

seconda volta. The second time.

segue. (1) Continue to the next movement without pausing; (2) continue in the same manner.

sehr. Very.

semplicità. Simplicity.

sempre. Always, continually.

sentimento. Sentiment, feeling.

senza. Without.

sforzando, sforzato (sfz, sf). With sudden emphasis.

sfumato. Diminishing and fading away.

simile. In a similar manner.

Singstimme. Singing voice.

sino al. Up to the . . . (usually followed by a new tempo marking, or by a dotted line indicating a terminal point).

smorzando (smorz.). Dying away.

sofort. Immediately.

solo (s.). Executed by one performer.

sonator. Player (*uno sonator,* one player; *due sonatori,* two players).

sonné à la double 8va. Play the double octave.

sopra. Above; in piano music, used to indicate that one hand must pass above the other.

soprano (S.). The voice classification with the highest range.

sordino (sord.). Mute.

sostenendo, sostenuto. Sustained.

sotto voce. In an undertone, subdued, under the breath.

sourdine. Mute.

soutenu. Sustained.

spiccato. With a light bouncing motion of the bow.

spiel. Play (an instrument).

spiritoso. In a spirited manner.

staccatissimo. Very staccato.

staccato (stacc.). Detached, separated, abruptly disconnected.

Stelle. Place; passage.

stentando, stentato (stent.). Delaying, retarding.

stesso movimento. The same basic pace.

stimm-. Voice.

Streicher. Bow

stretto. In a non-fugal composition, indicates a concluding section at an increased speed.

stringendo (string.). Quickening.

subito (sub.). Suddenly, immediately.

sul. On the (as in *sul G,* on the G string).

suono. Sound, tone.

superius. In older music, the uppermost part.

sur. On.

suspendue. Suspended.

tacet. The instrument or vocal part so marked is silent.

tasto solo. In a continuo part, this indicates that only the string instrument plays; the chord-playing instrument is silent.

tempo primo (tempo I). At the original tempo.

teneramente. Tenderly, gently.

tenor, tenore (T.). The highest male voice.

tenuto (ten.). Held, sustained.

tief. Deep, low.

tornando al tempo primo. Returning to the original tempo.

touch. Fingerboard (of a string instrument).

toujours. Always, continually.

tranquillo. Quietly, calmly.

tre corda (t.c.). Release the soft (or *una corda*) pedal of the piano.

tremolo (trem). On string instruments, a quick reiteration of the same tone, produced by a rapid up-and-down movement of the bow; also a rapid alternation between two different notes.

très. Very.

trill (tr.). The rapid alternation of a given note with the diatonic second above it. In a drum part it indicates rapid alternating strokes with two drumsticks.

triplum. In medieval polyphonic music, a voice part above the tenor.

troppo. Too much.

tutta la forza. Very emphatically.

tutti. Literally, "all"; usually means all the instruments in a given category as distinct from a solo part.

übergreifen. To overlap.

übertönend. Drowning out.

una corda (u.c.). With the "soft" pedal of the piano depressed.

und. And.

unison (unis.). The same notes or melody played by several instruments at the same pitch. Often used to emphasize that a phrase is not to be divided among several players.

verhallend. Fading away.

verklingen lassen. To let die away.

verlöschend. Extinguishing.

vierhändig. Four-hand piano music.

viertel. Quarter (*Viertelnote,* quarternote; *Viertelton,* quarter tone).

vif. Lively.

vigoroso. Vigorous, strong.

vivace. Quick, lively.

vivo. Lively.

voce. Voice (as in *colla voce,* a direction for the accompaniment to follow the solo part in tempo and expression).

voilà. There.

vorbereiten. To prepare in advance.

Vorhang auf. Curtain up.

Vorhang fällt, Vorhang zu. Curtain down.

vorher. Beforehand; previously.
voriges. Preceding.

Walzertempo. In the tempo of a waltz.
weg. Away, beyond.
weich. Mellow, smooth, soft.
weiter. Further, forward.
werden. Become; grow.
wie aus der Ferne. As if from afar.
wieder. Again.
wie oben. As above, as before.
wie zu Anfang dieser Szene. As at the beginning of this scene.

wüthend. Furiously.

zart. Tenderly, delicately.
Zeitmass. Tempo.
zögernd. Slower.
zu. The phrases *zu 2, zu 3* (etc.) indicate that the part is to be played in unison by 2, 3 (etc.) players.
zurückhaltend. Slackening in speed.
zurücktreten. To withdraw.
zweihändig. With two hands.

Index of Forms and Genres

A roman numeral following a title indicates a movement within the work named.